MOMENTS OF LOVE

How long Pierre kissed her she had no idea.

She knew only that the rapture and ecstasy of it was out of time and might have lasted a few seconds or many centuries.

"I did not know . . . I never guessed a . . . kiss could be so wonderful . . . so perfect!"

"Is that what it was for you?" he asked.

"It was like the . . . moonlight . . . like the . . . light you try to paint . . . now I understand what it . . . means to you."

Simonetta's voice trembled with the intensity of her feelings, and after a moment he said:

"You have never been kissed before?"

"No . . . of course . . . not."

Then he was kissing her again, his lips passionate, insistent, demanding, and she surrendered herself to him so completely that she felt as if her body melted into his. . . .

Moments of Love

Barbara Cartland

Moments of Love

First Published in United States 1982
© 1982 Barbara Cartland
This Edition Published by **Book Essentials South** 1999
Distributed by **BMI**, Ivyland, PA 18974
PRINTED IN THE UNITED STATES OF AMERICA
ISBN 1-57723-420-0

Author's Note

The term "Impressionism" was invented by a minor journalist, but Jean Corot used the word to define his conception of painting, saying:

"The beautiful in art is truth bathed in the *Impression* we have received when confronting nature."

Instead of representing forms as they exist in their defined and unchangeable structure, the Impressionists wished to interpret them as they appeared to them at a given moment.

The essential point of their art is to paint instinctively "as birds sing," and the result suggested by light and colour creates the illusion of the animation of life.

Of Claude Monet, 1840–1926, the leader of the Impressionist Movement, it was said:

"He came and unsealed the doors of light."

"We are in the presence of living nature, conquered and subdued by this miraculous painter."

Alfred Sisley, whose works I admire the most, never achieved fame or fortune and spent a life of abject poverty, selling his works at trifling prices. He died of cancer of the throat in 1899, and within three years his works commanded high prices.

Chapter One

1880

Lady Simonetta Terrington-Trench ran up the steps of the great Mansion where she had lived all her life, entered the huge marble Hall, and ran past the two footmen on duty.

They had been whispering to each other until she appeared, then they quickly straightened themselves to assume the passive expressions which were considered correct.

"Where is His Grace?" Lady Simonetta asked over her shoulder as she passed them swiftly.

"In the Study, M'Lady," one replied.

Lady Simonetta said nothing, and it was indeed doubtful if she had really listened to the man's answer, because she was already certain that her father would be in the Study.

She sped down a long corridor decorated with ancient suits of armour and the shields and weapons of bygone years when the Trenches were continually at war, either with their own enemies or those of their country.

Bursting open the door of the Study, which was her father's private room and where he did not welcome

1

guests, she found him, as she had hoped, at his desk. He was not writing but placing some papers in a long thin case.

He looked up in surprise, then smiled when he saw who the intruder was.

The Duke was extremely fond of his only daughter, who, he thought privately, was growing more beautiful day by day.

A handsome man, the Duke had always been known as having an eye for a pretty woman as well as for a horse, and he thought now, with a little pang in his heart, that it was only a question of time before Simonetta was married to a suitable husband and lost to him.

"Papa!" Simonetta cried breathlessly as she ran towards him. "I want you to see what I have just painted. I am sure you will think it is better than anything I have done before."

As she reached him, she held out towards him a small square canvass she was holding in her hands.

The Duke took it from her.

He looked down at it, carefully taking in every stroke of the artwork.

Simonetta watched his face anxiously until he said:

"Very good—much the best you have done—and you have captured the light in a way which I could not have done better myself."

Simonetta gave a cry of delight as she asked:

"Do you really mean that, Papa? Do you really think it is good?"

"Very good," replied the Duke.

"I am so pleased. I knew you were disappointed with the last picture I did. Suddenly I felt this one come right, almost as if . . . someone was guiding my hand."

The Duke laughed.

"That is what we always hope will happen. But in the end it depends only on our own efforts and our unceasing endeavours towards perfection."

Simonetta smiled at him as if she understood exactly what he was saying.

Then she glanced down at the long, flat case on his desk and was suddenly still.

"What are you doing? You are . . . going away?"

The Duke could not meet her eyes, and she exclaimed:

"You are! Oh, Papa, you cannot leave me now! Just when there are so many exciting things to paint in the garden!"

"I shall be away only about two weeks," the Duke replied, "and you will have your Aunt Harriet here to look after you."

"That is not true," Simonetta answered. "I thought you knew that Aunt Harriet sent a note by a groom yesterday, saying that unfortunately she had to go to London and would not be coming to stay as we had expected."

The Duke's lips tightened.

"Why was I not told last night?"

"The note was lying in the Hall, and as it was opened I thought you must have seen it."

There was a pause, then the Duke said:

"I remember now. The note arrived, and then before I could read it I was called away to deal with something else."

There was silence, then Simonetta said in a very small voice:

"Could I not . . . come with . . . you?"

"No, of course not," the Duke answered quickly. "I am going to France."

"Again?" Simonetta questioned. "You are going to paint, Papa, where this time?"

Again the Duke looked a little uncomfortable.

"As a matter of fact," he said, "I am going to Provence. I have been lent a small house at a place called Les Baux, where I am told the light is different from that anywhere else."

"I have read that also. Les Baux is one of the most exciting places in France," Simonetta said. "You will remember that we have often talked about the Troubadours who wrote their poems and songs at the Courts of Love."

"That was many years ago," the Duke remarked.

"Yes, I know," Simonetta answered, "but the ruins are still there amongst the volcanic rocks, and it is something I would like to see more than anything else in the world."

The Duke, still sitting at his desk, rustled his papers.

"Perhaps you will be able to go there one day. I will meet some of my painter friends who have no idea who I am except that they know I am trying to emulate their new concept of art."

"I am sure they will find you a very good Impressionist, Papa, but you know that no-one in England will appreciate your work any more than they appreciate what your friend Claude Monet is showing in France."

It was the French painter Claude Monet who had first inspired the Duke, who always said that he himself just dabbled on canvass to try to imitate the Impressionist style of painting.

Monet had been staying in England when the Duke had met him at an Exhibition. Strangely enough, they had become friends.

Monet was not so controversial as some of the other Impressionists, but his canvasses were more often rejected than accepted by the Salons.

Simonetta knew that it amused her father to slip away to Paris for about a week at a time, or a little longer, to mix with the Impressionist painters to whom Claude Monet introduced him.

Because the Duke was accepted amongst them as a painter and not an aristocrat, he travelled under an assumed name and no-one except Monet had any idea of his importance in England.

As Simonetta loved art of every kind, she was trying to copy the style her father admired.

He had told her a great deal about the Impressionists and their work, and already she was a devoted disciple of the style that Monet and his friends were trying to get recognised.

Simonetta, with a note in her voice that her father always found difficult to resist, pleaded:

"Please . . . Papa, take me . . . with you just . . . this once."

The Duke did not reply and she went on:

"Otherwise I shall be alone here, now that Aunt Harriet cannot come."

"I cannot leave you alone. You will have to go to one of your other aunts. You know Louise is always ready to have you."

Simonetta gave a little cry of protest.

"I refuse, I absolutely refuse to go to Aunt Louise! The moment I arrive she will be cross-examining me about every young man I have ever met, and then she will try to foist some abominable protégé of her own on me as a husband."

There was a scowl between the Duke's eyes as he listened.

He was well aware that his sister Louise was continually match-making in one way or another, and he had no wish to press Simonetta into marriage too soon or to force her to marry someone she did not love.

Unlike most aristocrats, whose marriages were arranged for the convenience of their families, the Duke had married for love.

He had been extremely happy with his wife, and despite numerous gloomy forecasts that he would soon be looking round for another woman, he had been unswervingly faithful to her.

Only after the Duchess had died some eight years ago, when Simonetta was only ten, had he allowed himself to be consoled by the many lovely ladies who had always found him exceedingly attractive.

He therefore had no intention of pressurising his sons into marriage, and he was even more determined that his daughter, whom he adored, should follow the dictates of her own heart.

He could see all too clearly that Simonetta was growing more and more like her mother and, at the same time, as beautiful as the woman for whom she had been named.

It was on their honeymoon in Florence that the Duke and his wife had looked at Botticelli's exquisite canvass in the Uffizi Gallery and the Duchess had said in her soft voice:

"If we ever have a daughter, Clyde darling, I pray she will be as beautiful as Botticelli's *Venus*."

"Botticelli's model was Simonetta Vespucci," the Duke had replied. "It has always been my favourite painting, and when I first saw you I thought you resembled her."

"You could not say anything more flattering," his wife had answered, "and one day I will give you a Simonetta of your own."

They had three sons first, and then when the Duchess had almost despaired of having more children, Simonetta had arrived.

The fact that she had red-gold hair like the original Simonetta and that her features were perfect and her eyes as soft, gentle, and sensitive as those of Botticelli's *Venus* seemed to both the Duke and the Duchess a miracle.

Yet, looking at his daughter now, the Duke felt that beauty could sometimes bring penalties, and without his wife to help him he was afraid of what might happen to Simonetta now that she had grown up.

"Papa... please... please!" she was pleading.

She had the feeling that although for a moment he did not speak, the Duke was weakening in his resolve to leave her behind.

"It is quite impossible," he said at length, "because as you know, I travel incognito."

"I can be incognito too," Simonetta replied.

"I can hardly arrive with a daughter I have never mentioned before, and quite frankly, dearest, some of the painters I shall meet in Les Baux are not the type of men I should introduce to you."

Simonetta laughed.

"I shall be quite safe with you, Papa, and if to have your daughter with you would cramp your style, I could pretend to be somebody else."

It flashed through the Duke's mind that if he arrived with a very pretty girl, it would certainly not surprise his Impressionist friends!

Indeed, quite certainly they would suspect what his interest in her was.

"I know!" Simonetta exclaimed. "I will come as your pupil! All great painters have pupils. No-one would think it at all strange that you should have one too."

"A pupil?" the Duke repeated slowly.

"Why not?" Simonetta asked. "You know we were discussing only the other night that Rubens and Rembrandt had dozens of pupils who helped them with their work and copied their style to the best of their ability."

"That was different," the Duke answered. "Both Rubens and Rembrandt were extremely popular painters and had so many commissions that they were unable to complete every detail of a painting themselves."

"Why not be optimistic and think that is what will happen to you in a few years?" Simonetta suggested. "Then I shall obviously be very useful to you."

The Duke laughed.

"You are trying to coax me into something I know I should not do," he said. "Quite frankly, Simonetta, however much pressure you may put upon me, I intend to leave you behind."

"With Aunt Louise?" Simonetta asked. "Very well, if

you do, on your return you will find me engaged to some nauseating Marquis or pretentious Prince and it will be all your fault."

"It is ridiculous to talk like that," the Duke said sharply. "I have no intention of allowing you to marry anyone until you have had a chance to look round and find a man with whom you will be very happy."

"At the moment, I am only really happy with you, Papa."

Simonetta walked round the desk, and standing behind her father put her arms round his neck. Then she laid her cheek against his and said:

"Please take me with you, Papa! It will be such fun to be together. I promise I will do exactly as you tell me and not get involved with any man of whom you disapprove."

There was no response.

Simonetta tightened her arms round him a little bit more before she said:

"You would be looking after me, and I know Mama would want me to look after you."

The Duke capitulated.

"Very well. I will take you with me. But if you get into any trouble or if there is any unpleasantness, I shall bring you home immediately. Do you understand?"

Simonetta did not answer because she was kissing his cheek.

"Thank you, Papa!" she said between kisses. "Thank you . . . thank you . . . I love you and we will have a wonderful time together!"

* * *

Travelling towards Paris, Simonetta was enjoying an adventure which was more exciting than anything she had ever done before in her life.

In the past, when her father had gone away, she had always been left in the charge of Governesses or some elderly relative who spent the time lecturing her or finding fault.

Because her father meant everything in her life, she would count the days until his return, and then would wait for hours, watching the drive for the first sign of the horses which were bringing him home.

After the boredom and monotony of lessons and more lessons, she would spend the day with her father, riding over the Estate, fishing on the lake, and dining with him in the evening.

More than anything else she enjoyed the conversations they had and the occasions when they vied with each other in painting some particular view or one of the statues with which the garden abounded.

It was her father who had first told her about the light which the Impressionists had introduced into the paintings, and it was this which had altered her whole conception of art.

She had listened intently to his lectures and then tried to emulate the way he painted, and with the loyalty of a child she admired his paintings more than those of the great Masters which hung in the house.

Previous members of the family had contributed to a large and important collection which was famous over the whole world.

It was not surprising that the Duke, brought up amongst some of the finest paintings in existence, had himself wanted to paint.

However, it had been merely a hobby and few of his relations had sympathised or thought it interesting.

Even the Duke himself had been only spasmodic in his attention to art, until he met Claude Monet.

After that, he visited Paris and became involved in and amused by a world which before he had not even realised existed.

It had made it more exciting that he met the Impressionists not as himself but merely as an aspiring painter to whom they could talk on equal terms.

Previously, when the Duke crossed the Channel he had stayed with his distinguished French friends and was taken to Soirées, Assemblies, Court Balls, and of course the exclusive and expensive "Houses of Pleasure."

The Impressionists, on the other hand, talked incessantly in cheap cafés, drank a great deal of absinth, and complained that they were not appreciated.

The Duke found that he had a great deal in common with the more distinguished of them to whom he was introduced by Monet.

In fact, he found himself looking forward to such trips as an oasis in the desert when he would be a struggling artist amongst others of his kind and could lay aside his more serious and certainly more distinguished responsibilities.

Now in the comfortable reserved carriage in which they were travelling to Paris, he looked at Simonetta and wondered if he was being extremely foolhardy in taking her with him.

It was a question he had asked himself quite a number of times before he had agreed to her almost preposterous suggestion that she should accompany him as his pupil.

But he had found it impossible to be so unkind as to leave her behind at a moment when, having just left the School-Room, she had few friends whom she could visit at a moment's notice.

He was also quite prepared to agree that she was right in maintaining that her Aunt Louise was not a suitable person with whom to stay in his absence.

There were, of course, a great number of other relations who would have been only too delighted to have her, but such arrangements took time to organise.

The Duke had been promised the house in Provence for only a limited period while the owner was away, and he had no wish to miss such an opportunity.

The owner, who was an Art Dealer and a friend of Monet, was a man who liked his comforts and the Duke was certain that the house might be small but would be comfortable.

It would certainly be better than staying in some small, cheap Hotel with other painters who shared rooms with one another and who often, after too many glasses of absinth, had to be helped upstairs.

This was a side of his new friends which he had no intention of introducing to Simonetta and which he himself found unpleasant and boring.

He quite seriously wanted to paint when he reached Les Baux, but he also found it congenial after the sunset to have men to talk to about the subject in which he was so interested.

He tried to ease his conscience by saying that no-one would know or guess that he and Simonetta were not what they pretended to be.

It was wildly exciting for Simonetta—like arranging a charade or giving a performance in the small Theatre attached to the Ducal Mansion.

There, she had for the last few years produced at Christmas a pantomime for the household and the children on the Estate.

The Duke had been very firm about how she was to look.

"Respectable, but poor," he said. "You are too interested in art to care much what you wear."

Simonetta laughed.

"It is not going to be easy, Papa. All my gowns were very expensive, and although a man may not be impressed by them, a woman certainly will."

"You will have to find something suitable or I will not take you with me," the Duke said firmly.

"I will find something very suitable," Simonetta promised demurely, but her eyes were twinkling.

It was not easy, but in the end she found several plain

gowns she had worn several years previously and had
the seamstress who worked in the Castle let them out
for her.

"Whatever do you want these old rags for, M'Lady?"
Mrs. Baines had asked. "If I'd had my way, I'd have
sent them to the Orphanage years ago."

"I shall be taking part in a play when I am away with
my Papa," Simonetta had replied. "I have to act the
role of a poor girl who has to earn her own living. Of
course, in the end she marries Prince Charming."

"You'll have plenty of gowns for the last scene," Mrs.
Baines had remarked.

The plain dresses were altered, and Simonetta also
used her imagination and had Mrs. Baines make her a
little blue velvet coat which she thought would be
exactly what artists would admire.

There was also just time to run up several soft
blouses with flowing bows at the neck!

As it all had to be done in a great hurry, the house-
maids helped and asked dozens of inquisitive questions
about the play.

By the time the Duke was ready to leave, Simonetta
had a small trunk full of clothes, and when she showed
them to him, he admitted that they would not arouse
much attention.

However, he forgot that they would look very different when Simonetta was wearing them. With her strange
red-gold hair and blue-green eyes, anything looked
sensational on her, however cheap or plain it might be
in reality.

He and Simonetta had left the country early in the
morning and gone to the house in London which was
for the moment shut up.

The Duke intended to open it when Simonetta was
presented to the Queen, after which he planned to give
a Ball for her.

That was more than a month ahead, and in the

meantime there were only a few elderly servants in charge of Faringham House in Park Lane, who were surprised to see them and relieved that they were intending to stay only an hour or so.

Because they were too old to be curious, they appeared not to notice that while the Duke and Simonetta arrived with quite a number of pieces of luggage, most of them were left in their bedrooms.

When they departed they had only two small trunks with them and they looked very different from when they had arrived from the country.

The Duke sent his carriage away and they took a hackney-carriage to Victoria Station.

He told Simonetta that from now on they would, in effect, be taking part in a play on the stage.

"We must forget our real identities and 'think ourselves' into the characters and personalities we have assumed."

"I will try, Papa!" Simonetta replied with a smile.

"I do not intend to be uncomfortable until we actually reach our destination," the Duke went on, "even if some people think we may look a little strange as First Class passengers."

As he was so distinguished and so handsome, Simonetta thought it would be impossible for him to look anything but a gentleman.

But she noticed that he was treated quite differently as plain Mr. Calvert—which was what he called himself—than as His Grace, the Duke of Faringham.

The Station Master, in a braided uniform and a top-hat, did not see them off at Victoria, nor were they escorted onto the ship in which they crossed the Channel by the Officer in charge of the Port.

A porter found their reserved carriage for them and said:

"*Merci beaucoup, M'sieur,*" for the *pourboire* he received, then he hurried away.

There were no officials, no secretaries, and no valets to see to their comfort, but Simonetta knew that her father was enjoying the freedom of being on his own.

"You are like a School-boy playing truant, Papa," she teased.

"I am waited on, cosseted, and fussed over every day I am alive," the Duke replied. "I admit, Simonetta, that I find it rather fun to be an ordinary man amongst ordinary men."

"It is very, very exciting for me too!"

"Now you behave yourself," the Duke admonished. "Otherwise I shall have no compunction about taking you home immediately and admitting I made a mistake in letting you travel with me."

"You know as well as I do, Papa, you like having me with you," Simonetta answered. "While for me it is a wonderful, wonderful adventure!"

She paused before she asked:

"Do you think I look pretty enough to be your pupil?"

The Duke wanted to reply: "much too pretty," but he thought it might make her self-conscious and instead answered casually:

"You look all right."

He had already make up his mind that she must stay at the house in the evening and not come to the Inn or wherever else the other painters met when it was too dark to go on painting.

He knew that Simonetta would be quite happy to be alone with a book—in fact, her Governesses and her aunts had always complained that she read too much.

"I will be with her most of the time," the Duke decided. "But it would be a mistake for her to mix with my rather strange friends. She must stay at home and read."

He had it all planned out in his mind, and he had to admit that secretly he enjoyed having his daughter with him.

Because Simonetta was intelligent, she stimulated his mind, and he thought that when he was talking to her he often forgot she was not his contemporary.

He was very fond of his sons and they had close bonds in common with their sporting interests, especially when it concerned horses and shooting.

But with Simonetta he had an affinity on the more intellectual and spiritual subjects about which he had never talked with another woman except his wife.

Looking at her, with her eyes alight with excitement and her straight little nose silhouetted against the carriage as she stared out the window, the Duke wondered what would happen to her in life and felt a pang of desperate anxiety in case she was ever made unhappy.

He realised more than anyone else how sensitive she was, how intuitive, while at the same time she had an irrepressible sense of humour.

'I will kill any man who hurts her,' he thought.

He tried to tell himself that she was still too young to be concerned with men, but he knew in his heart that when she appeared on the social scene, men would certainly be concerned with her and that was when the trouble would begin.

With a little sigh the Duke viewed the future rather apprehensively.

For the moment he had Simonetta to himself. He was the only man in her life, the man she admired, and at present there were no rivals.

The train rattled on and it was getting late.

Simonetta opened the picnic-basket that they had brought with them from Faringham Park.

"Delicious things to eat, Papa," she said. "Pâté, cold chicken, ham which has been cured just the way you like it, and a bottle of Champagne."

"I will open that right away," the Duke said. "I suppose you now think you are grown up and would like some too."

"Only to drink a toast to our adventure," Simonetta

replied. "Quite frankly I prefer lemonade, which I see Chef has remembered to include, besides some Marrons Glacés which I adore."

"I only hope that we have been left a good cook in the house where we shall be staying," the Duke said. "The food in French Inns is usually impregnated with garlic, and I doubt if you would appreciate frogs'-legs, which is one of the dishes for which Provence is famous."

Simonetta wrinkled her small nose for a moment, then she said:

"I think it is stupid for the British to dislike anything simply because it is different. I am determined to try frogs'-legs, snails, and truffles, and I shall refuse to eat them only if they taste nasty."

"That is very sensible of you," said the Duke. "At the same time, it is no use forcing oneself to like something just because it is new."

As he spoke he was thinking that perhaps because they were different from the people she had met before, Simonetta would have an idealistic conception of painters.

Now he kept remembering things about his acquaintances in the Art World, some of whom would undoubtedly be at Les Baux!

Some were men of loose morals, and certainly from a lady's point of view they were undesirable characters.

'I should not have brought Simonetta with me,' the Duke thought for the hundredth time.

But it was too late to have regrets.

However, it would be a cruelty he could not possibly contemplate to leave her in Paris with some respectable French family with whom she would undoubedly be extremely bored, or to send her back to England to be with his sister Louise.

He drank some of the Champagne, and then raising his glass he said:

"To ourselves, Simonetta, you and I—may we have a golden holiday together!"

"I know we shall, Papa," Simonetta replied. "I drink to you, an Impressionist and the most adorable man in the whole world."

"Thank you!"

Father and daughter smiled at each other with an understanding which they both would have found impossible to explain in words.

They stayed the night in Paris in a quiet Hotel near the Bois, which was very different from the houses in which the Duke stayed when he travelled as himself.

Then, a comfortable carriage with a coachman and a footman on the box would meet him at the station and drive him either to a huge Mansion in the Champs Élysées or to a bachelor-apartment where he was the guest of one of his more raffish friends.

He would have a host to welcome him, a profusion of invitations already waiting for him to accept, and he would be taken for dinner either to a private party in some aristocrat's house or else to one of the famous Restaurants.

There the *elite* of Paris would be gathered, not with their wives but with the bejewelled, exquisitely gowned Courtesans for which the gayest city of Europe was famous.

The conversation would be witty with a *double entendre* in every sentence.

The food would be superlative, the wine excellent, and the Duke always knew exactly how the evening would end!

He remembered only too well the very glamorous woman with whom he had spent a great deal of his time the last time he had been in Paris.

He had been attracted to her because she had hair that somewhat resembled his wife's.

Now as he looked at Simonetta he realised that the

colour had been false and had come out of a dye-pot.

This time, he told himself, there would be no fakes as far as he and Simonetta were concerned, no disappointments, and no hangovers the morning after the night before to spoil the memories of their time together.

It would be a joy to her, as it would be a joy to him.

When the Duke fell asleep in the Hotel he thought that there was nothing else in the world he would rather do than what he was doing at the moment.

* * *

To Simonetta everything was new and very exciting.

Paris was exactly as she had imagined it would be.

The houses with their grey shutters, the trees in the Boulevards, the people sitting outside the cafés, the gaslights shining above them—all contributed to a feeling of exhilaration in the air which she could not exactly explain.

They had breakfast in their Sitting-Room the next morning before they left, but Simonetta found it impossible to eat anything because she kept running to the window to watch the people passing by and to look out through the trees over the grey roofs.

"Paris is so pretty, Papa," she kept saying. "I wish we were staying here a little while."

"I will bring you to Paris another time," the Duke promised, "and then you will see it in all its glory. You will drive in a smart carriage in the Bois and attend what will undoubtedly be a hot and crowded Reception in the Champs Élysées Palace."

"That does not sound half as exciting as what we are doing now," Simonetta replied. "But I wish we could go and sit outside at the cafés and tonight watch the dancers in one of the Dancing-Halls I have read about."

"Certainly not," the Duke said firmly. "And you had better put on your hat and strap up your trunk or we shall miss our train."

"I had forgotten I had to do that myself," Simonetta
said with a laugh, and left him to run to her own room.

She found it strange to manage without a lady's-maid
and thought it very clever of her father to look after
himself without Jarvis, who had valeted him ever since
she could remember and who had always behaved
rather like a disapproving Nanny.

'Jarvis would certainly not fit in on this trip,' Simonetta
thought with a smile.

Now she locked her trunk, did up the straps, and put
on her plain hat, its only trimming a small quill, on her
shining hair.

Then she put on a travelling-cape which was in a
subdued shade of blue.

If her father wished to make her look unobtrusive he
had failed, for it was a perfect frame for her clear, very
white skin and it also accentuated the red lights in her
fair hair.

"I think I look rather pretty," Simonetta told her
reflection in the mirror.

Then she was ashamed of being conceited and made
a little grimace which was something that certainly
would not have been approved of by any of her
Governesses.

Then she went dancing back to the Sitting-Room to
tell her father she was ready.

When they reached the station, the Duke said:

"I have taken a reserved carriage, although I hope
none of the people who are staying at Les Baux will see
us! But we have to change at Arles."

"What is wrong with a reserved carriage, Papa?"
Simonetta asked.

"Nothing," he replied, "except it is something that
could not be afforded by an Impressionist who has not
sold a painting for at least six months."

Simonetta laughed.

"Are we supposed to live on what we make?"

"In case they should be curious, we should have to

admit to a very small allowance and an income from other sources," the Duke replied.

"What are those?" Simonetta asked.

"I have not the slightest idea!"

They both laughed.

It was, however, a relief to have a comfortable carriage to themselves.

The picnic-basket which they had procured from the Hotel was not nearly as palatable as the one they had enjoyed the previous day, but there was a bottle of claret which the Duke found excellent and of which Simonetta had a sip or two.

They had started early but it was still a very long journey to Arles.

In fact, by the time they arrived, Simonetta was feeling tired and the Duke had dozed off several times during the afternoon.

"It is too late to go on tonight," he decided. "We will stay here and then drive to Les Baux in the morning."

Simonetta was too tired to argue, and they went to what the Duke was told was the best Hotel in the town, and they were thankful to be allotted two small and rather uncomfortable bedrooms as the rest of the place was full.

"What is happening that there should be so many people here?" Simonetta asked.

"I expect there is to be a Bull Fight," the Duke replied.

She gave a cry of horror.

"A Bull Fight! I have always thought it must be a very cruel, unpleasant sport."

"It is," the Duke agreed. "But the bulls in this part of the world are bred especially for fighting, and you will never persuade the local people to give up what to them is a traditional sport going back to the Romans."

"I have no wish to see it."

"Nor have I," her father answered, "so do not worry about it."

Because she was tired, she did not worry about anything and fell asleep.

In the morning, while the Duke was waiting for his *petit déjeuner* to be brought to his room, Simonetta burst in on him and said:

"Do you know there is a marvellous Amphitheatre here almost as fine as the Colosseum in Rome? We must see it!"

"Of course," the Duke agreed. "There is plenty of time for you to see the sights before we travel on to Les Baux."

"Do you mean that?" Simonetta cried. "You are kind! Although you may have seen everything before, it is very, very exciting for me."

"I think you will find Les Baux exciting too," the Duke said.

The maid arrived at that moment with his breakfast, and Simonetta did not have to answer as she was looking out the window.

She looked out on the narrow street where the ancient houses were filled with people who, she thought, seemed as strange as if they had come from a different planet from the one to which she belonged.

Then she had a strange feeling that this was the beginning of something new and stupendous in her life. It was almost as if fate or destiny beckoned to her.

She knew that as she went on there would be new horizons that she did not even know existed. New ideas seemed to flutter in the air which she could not grasp but yet was acutely aware of them.

The feeling she had in herself was so strange, yet it was undeniably there.

She told herself that the curtain was rising and this was where she would begin to live in a way she had never lived before.

Chapter Two

"This is very exciting for me!" Simonetta said as they set off in the open carriage drawn by two horses.

The Duke smiled.

"I feel the same, and whatever else happens, it will be an adventure we will share together."

Simonetta slipped her hand into his.

"A very thrilling adventure!" she said with a note in her voice that the Duke found very touching.

They were driving North-Eastwards from Arles towards Les Alpilles, a minature but remarkably wild mountain-range less than ten miles distant, where Les Baux lay perched on a rocky spur of the hills.

As soon as they were away from the traffic and the environs of the city, which Simonetta learnt had been founded as a Colony by Julius Caesar and had been both a Port and a busy market since the Sixth Century, she began to appreciate the landscape, which was different from anything she had seen before.

On one side of them, hidden by high hedges against the wind, there were market-gardens. When the ground began to rise, the lavender which she had been told was a speciality of Provence stood out dark purple amidst the slender almond trees.

They went on, and now there were golden crops, emerald-green meadows, trellised vines, and silver-grey olives.

"It is lovely! Is it not lovely, Papa?" Simonetta kept exclaiming.

She knew that her father was looking at it with different eyes, seeking what his Impressionist friends had told him was the intensity of the light.

It was his friend Claude Monet who had become the undisputed leader of the new school of artists and had the conception that painting should be done entirely in the open air.

"Light and colour," he had said to those who would listen to him, "were given us by God, and why should we refuse such a gift?"

While at first his idea had been revolutionary, he had even succeeded in bringing Édouard Manet and Renoir round to his conception of painting, and the Duke could understand how Provence would appeal to them perhaps more than any other part of France.

To Simonetta it was all an enchantment, and when finally they had their first glimpse of jagged high rocks, bare and sharp in their outline, it was such a sensational picture against the blue of the sky that she was speechless with the wonder of it.

She knew too that her father was impressed and they were both thinking of the desperate fighting that had taken place in mediaeval times between the Lords of Baux and their enemies.

Their almost impregnable fortress had meant the death of those who attacked them.

But now there was no violence—only a magic which grew as they drew nearer and held them spellbound because it was different from anything they had ever seen before.

The horses climbed up a twisting road which led towards the summit where the ruins of a Castle were perched high on rocks that were bleached so white that it was almost impossible to distinguish where one ended and the other began.

Then they were descending on the other side to where between two huge cliffs of bare rocks there was a small sheltered valley.

There were only a few houses, and almost before Simonetta was expecting it their driver brought the carriage to a standstill outside a small house with a shallow sloping Roman-style red roof with half-rounded wiltes.

She knew this was characteristic of the houses of Provence.

As she looked at the very small garden brilliant with flowers and the windows open to the sunshine, she thought it was like a doll's-house and very different from any other Mansion in which she had lived with her father.

"Is this where we are staying?" she asked in a low voice.

"I imagine so," the Duke replied.

They stepped from the carriage and walked along a small path to find that the door to the house was open.

They walked in and Simonetta saw that her father was so tall that his head almost touched the heavily beamed ceiling.

They had just time to look round and realise they were in a comfortable, well-furnished Sitting-Room, when a woman appeared through another door which doubtless led to the kitchen.

"*Bonjour, Monsieur,*" she said. "I imagine you're the guests that *Monsieur* Louis Gautier told me to expect."

"We are!" the Duke replied. "I am Clyde Calvert, and this is my—my pupil, *Mademoiselle* Simonetta."

"I am Marie," the woman answered. "*Monsieur* Gautier employs me to keep the house clean and tidy for him. If you want extra services, *Monsieur,* you must pay for them!"

She spoke aggressively, as if she was used to people expecting something for nothing.

"I am perfectly prepared to do that," the Duke replied, "and *Monsieur* Gautier informed me that you are a good cook."

"It depends what I have to cook with, *Monsieur*," Marie replied, again somewhat truculently.

The Duke put his hand in his pocket and drew out several golden *louis*.

"Let me give you your wages in advance, Marie," he said, "and also some money for food. And may I add that *Mademoiselle* and I like the best the countryside can produce."

Simonetta thought that Marie looked at the *louis* in her father's hand somewhat greedily before she replied:

"Bread's cheap, *Monsieur*, but the best butter, eggs, and chickens come expensive."

"I want you to buy the best, Marie," the Duke insisted.

He counted several *louis* into her hand, which she grasped quickly, almost as if she felt they might disappear and were merely part of her imagination.

In a very different tone she said:

"I'll do my best to please you, *Monsieur*. I'm considered one of the best cooks in Les Baux, so you'll not be disappointed."

"Thank you, Marie," the Duke said. "*Mademoiselle* and I will look forward to sampling your best culinary efforts at dinner, but now if it is possible we would appreciate a light luncheon."

"I'll make you an omelette, *Monsieur*, with the herbs of Provence, and tonight you shall taste my chicken with tarragon, which makes *Monsieur* Gautier kiss his fingers when he speaks of it."

The Duke smiled.

"I shall look forward to it, Marie."

He then turned to give instructions to the coachman who was bringing in their luggage.

There was a comfortable bedroom on the ground floor, which Simonetta insisted should be her father's, while she climbed a narrow staircase to where there was a small but prettily furnished bedroom under the sloping roof.

She liked it because she could look out at the high rocks on either side of the house.

Even at first glance she knew that the light on their bare surfaces was mesmeric and she wanted to go on looking, feeling that they stirred her in a way which no view had ever done before.

But she knew that her father was waiting for her downstairs, and after quickly unpacking one of her dresses she changed from the gown in which she had been travelling into one that was cool, then hurried down to the Sitting-Room.

As she expected, the Duke was unpacking his canvasses, paints, and easel, and she knew that he was already itching to be outside painting in the light that he had come so far to find.

It was quite difficult to persuade him to wait until he had eaten something first before he set off in search of inspiration.

Although Simonetta enjoyed the omelette with its special herbs that were different from any she had tasted before, she was aware that her father's eyes kept straying to the window.

His mind was already planning the picture he wished to translate onto canvass.

"I wish we could find a book that would tell us more about the Courts of Love," Simonetta said, in an effort to distract his attention from the view.

He answered absent-mindedly, and she knew that when he was in this mood he was full concentrated on his painting.

As soon as he had eaten the omelette and the delicious goat's-milk cheese which was made locally he jumped up from the table.

Without inviting Simonetta to go with him, he set off carrying his easel, stool, paints, and canvass, and disappeared down the dusty track which led towards the high rocks which she also was longing to explore.

But she realised it would be more sensible first to unpack and settle herself in the house, and she also thought she should get to know Marie.

She went to find her in the small, spotlessly clean kitchen, where, having been well paid for her services, Marie was now in a genial and receptive mood.

"Are you also a painter, *M'mselle?*" she enquired. "Or have you come to Provence to be with the handsome gentleman who's the friend of *Monsieur* Gautier?"

She asked the question in a way which seemed to Simonetta uncomfortably inquisitive, although she could not exactly explain why, and she replied quickly:

"*Monsieur* Calvert is my teacher and I am his pupil. I am very anxious to be a good painter."

Marie looked at her and Simonetta thought she was searching her face to find out if she was telling the truth. Then she said:

"*Tiens!* If there are not enough men wasting their time in painting without women copying them!"

Simonetta laughed.

"That is unfair! If women have talents, why should they not be allowed to use them?"

"The best thing for a woman to do," Marie said sharply, "is to bring up healthy children, and that leaves no time for anything else."

"How many children have you?"

"I have six," Marie replied, "and now that they are old enough to look after themselves, I can earn a little money in my spare time."

"That is what I shall be able to do if I become a successful painter," Simonetta remarked.

Marie put down the sauce-pan she was cleaning.

"With your looks, *M'mselle*," she said, "you ought to be able to find yourself a rich husband, whether or not you have a dowry. It is difficult for a girl who is plain, but if she is pretty enough there is always some man ready to make a fool of himself over her."

Simonetta laughed.

She could understand Marie's reasoning, which she intended as a compliment.

"I have no wish to be married at the moment," she said. "I had better unpack now and try to get some work done before the light fades."

"You will have plenty of time to paint before that happens," Marie said in a somewhat disparaging voice.

Going up the narrow staircase to her bedroom, Simonetta thought with a smile that Marie was like the critics in Paris who did not think much of Impressionists, nor did the public who would not buy their paintings.

Simonetta remembered that in the newspaper they had bought in Paris, a critic had written that "Monet and Renoir appear to be declaring war on beauty."

"How can they be so blind?" Simonetta had asked angrily when she read it.

"It is always the same with new ideas," the Duke had replied. "Ever since Galileo was imprisoned for saying that the world was round instead of flat, there have always been those who fight fanatically against new knowledge and new ideas."

Simonetta looked out the window at the tall rocks of Les Baux.

In the afternoon sunshine they were an exquisite gold and she wondered how anybody could fail to appreciate the luminosity of them.

The light which made the Impressionists paint in a different way from all those before them was, she thought, something which was seen not only by the eyes but by the innermost instincts of the soul.

"I must try to paint in the same way," she told herself.

She hurriedly hung her gowns in a cupboard, ran downstairs to pack up her paint-box and a small canvass, then went out into the garden at the front of the house.

There was really no need to go any farther to find a subject for her to paint other than the house with its warm red roof silhouetted against the bare rocks peaking to the sky.

It was so beautiful that it held her and made her feel as if she felt its loveliness deep in her heart.

Her father had brought a second small easel with him, which she had seen propped in a corner of the Sitting-Room, and she knew it was something she could borrow.

She fetched it and set it up in front of a large stone that was half-covered with moss, and after mixing her colours she tried to set down on canvass the contrast of light and shade which the Impressionists knew was a visual impression of life itself.

Her father had explained to her in simple terms what they were trying to achieve.

"Whatever else it is," he had said, "Impressionism is first and foremost a way of seeing."

"They see light as life?" Simonetta had asked.

"Exactly!" her father replied. "And it was the magic of light conveyed by the magic of colour which in the beginning became the guiding-point of the first Impressionists."

He saw that Simonetta was trying to follow him and he went on:

"It is the light which gives life to colour, and the Impressionists such as Monet paint the colours they see, not those which they are told belong to this or that object."

"I think I understand," Simonetta said.

Her father had helped her by asking her what colours she saw in this tree or in that wood, and gradually she found that almost every colour was complementary to another.

And she soon discovered that every object took on a

strange and different colour according to the light in which one looked at it.

"I understand," Simonetta said to herself after that, "but it is still very difficult to portray light in ordinary paints, and I need magic ones which will change as quickly as the light itself!"

Nevertheless she tried, and after painting for nearly two hours she thought she had at last begun to get something on the canvass of which her father would approve.

Because she had begun to feel very hot with the sun beating down on her bare head all the time she had been working, she went into the house in search of shade.

Sitting down in a comfortable armchair, she must have fallen asleep, for when she awoke it was late in the afternoon and her father was just coming in through the door.

"Oh, Papa, you are back already!" she exclaimed.

"I have come back because the heat of the sun has made me thirsty," her father explained.

"Shall I make you some tea?" Simonetta asked. "Or shall I find out if there is any wine in the house?"

"I think I should like that later when I go to the Inn," the Duke replied, "so tea will do at the moment, although I would prefer something cool."

Simonetta went into the kitchen, and while the kettle was boiling she found a lemon which Marie must have brought with her. Squeezing it into a glass, she took it to her father, who drank thirstily.

"I wonder what fruits we can buy," he said. "I noticed as we were coming along that the cherries which are usually the first to appear were red amongst the leaves."

"I saw plenty of olives," Simonetta said, "but I do not believe they would make a very exciting drink."

As she spoke there was the sound of footsteps outside

the front door, and they both looked round in surprise as a man walked into the house.

He was dark, obviously a Frenchman, and very smartly dressed in riding-clothes, his boots so highly polished that they seemed to mirror his surroundings.

"*Bonjour.* Is Louis Gautier here?" he asked in French.

The Duke rose slowly to his feet.

"No, he is in Paris," he replied. "I am a friend of his, and he has lent me his house."

The Frenchman smiled.

"If Gautier has done that, then I am certain you are an artist."

"I try to be," the Duke replied. "My name is Clyde Calvert."

The Frenchman looked at him, his eyes narrowing contemplatively before he said:

"I gather from the way you speak that you are English, *Monsieur,* and I believe I have heard Gautier speak of you. I think he has sold some of your paintings."

"When I have anything to sell," the Duke replied drily.

The Frenchman laughed.

"Most painters say: 'until I have the opportunity of selling.' I understand that the market is bad, but from an artist's point of view, when has it ever been anything else?"

The Duke did not reply, and Simonetta realised that the Frenchman was looking not at her father but at her.

"Let me introduce myself," he said after a moment. "I am the *Comte* Jacques de Laval. I am a Patron of the Arts and, as Gautier will confirm, a very good customer of his."

The Duke inclined his head at the introduction, but he did not say anything and after a moment the *Comte* said:

"Will you not introduce me to *Mademoiselle?*"

"This is my—my pupil," the Duke said quickly. "Her name is Simonetta."

"Very suitable," the *Comte* remarked. "She undoubtedly has an uncanny resemblance to her namesake."

He moved towards Simonetta as he spoke, and she held out her hand. He did not shake it as she expected, but instead raised it to his lips.

"*Enchanté, Mademoiselle,*" he said, "and as you are a painter, I hope you will allow me to see your work."

"There is not very much of it," Simonetta answered quickly.

The *Comte* laughed.

"I would be interested in anything *you* have produced."

It was so obviously a compliment that Simonetta looked at her father.

To her surprise, instead of looking annoyed that the *Comte* should seek her attention, he was smiling and exclaimed:

"Laval! Now I know where I have heard your name. You bought a painting of Claude Monet's last year. He told me about it, and it was a great honour that you should add it to your collection."

"I am a great admirer of Monet," the *Comte* said.

"As I am," the Duke agreed.

Without being invited, the *Comte* sat down in a chair and in a moment they were deep in a discussion on Monet's work.

"He has discovered the power of light," the Duke said. "Could anything more be said of this extraordinary man?"

"No, indeed," the *Comte* agreed.

As he was talking his eyes kept roving towards Simonetta, and she had the feeling that he was talking to her father simply so that he could prolong the opportunity of looking at her.

She thought that perhaps it was her imagination, but

the *Comte*'s dark eyes and the expression in them made her feel shy, so she rose to her feet and went to the kitchen to see if the kettle was boiling.

"Your pupil is very young," the *Comte* said to the Duke, bringing the conversation abruptly away from Monet.

"Very young," the Duke replied briefly. "I only brought her with me because she has an outstanding talent which would be a mistake to waste."

"Of course, of course!" the *Comte* agreed.

As Simonetta came back with a tray on which she had placed a pot of tea and three cups, he said:

"I am very anxious, *Monsieur* Calvert, to show you and your pupil my collection of paintings, quite a number of which I keep here in my *Château*, although of course I have many more in Paris."

The Duke hesitated.

"We are here only for a short time," he said after a moment, "and wish to paint as much as we can while we are in Les Baux."

"I promise I shall not encroach on your painting time," the *Comte* said with a smile, "so I will invite you to dinner. If you and *Mademoiselle* Simonetta will dine with me tomorrow night, I will not only send a carriage for you but will also show you Monet's *Summer,* which I bought six years ago."

"You bought that?" the Duke exclaimed. "It is certainly a painting I have always wished to see."

"It is hanging in my *Château* in a place of honour. There are also paintings by a number of other Impressionists such as Cézanne and Renoir, which I am sure you will find as lovely as I do."

It was an invitation, Simonetta knew, that her father could not resist. At the same time, she wondered a little apprehensively what she should wear.

The Duke had been insistent that she would not require any evening-gowns and that it would seem strange if she was even known to possess one.

As if he could sense what she was thinking, the *Comte* said:

"We will dine of course informally, and as I am quite certain you will be painting up until the very moment that the sun sinks, I will expect you and *Mademoiselle* to come just as you are."

"It is very kind of you," the Duke said sincerely, "and I do certainly wish to see Monet's *Summer*. It was sold before I was able to do so, and we have often talked about it."

"Then I will look forward to the pleasure of showing it to you," the *Comte* replied.

He refused the tea which Simonetta offered him and rose to his feet a little reluctantly.

"I have left my horse in the charge of a small boy," he said, "and I do not think I should trust him too far."

He held out his hand to the Duke.

"Au revoir," he said. "We will meet again tomorrow evening."

"Thank you," the Duke replied.

"The *Comte* took Simonetta's hand in his.

"Has anybody told you, *Mademoiselle*," he said, "that it would be difficult to find a more alluring subject to paint than your face and hair? Perhaps only Botticelli could do it justice."

"As an artist I am more interested in landscapes," Simonetta replied demurely.

"We must find somebody to paint you who has the use of both his eyes," the *Comte* answered.

Simonetta laughed. Then she said:

"I wish to be a painter, *Monsieur*, not a model."

"We will certainly have to discuss that further."

As he kissed her hand his lips rested for a moment on her skin, then he walked through the front door to be followed politely by the Duke to see him leave.

Simonetta rubbed her hand against her skirt.

She did not know why, but she thought that the touch of his lips made her feel a little creepy.

The Duke came back into the room.

"He was far too interested in you," he said as he picked up the cup of tea he had put down before he followed the *Comte*. "I have a good mind to make you stay behind when I dine with him tomorrow."

Simonetta gave a little cry of protest.

"But, Papa, I want to see the Monet! Have you really heard of the *Comte* before?"

"Yes, I have," the Duke replied. "He has bought many Impressionist paintings, and it has often been said in my hearing that he is generous to some artists."

"Then I imagine he is very rich," Simonetta said, "because from what you have always told me, Papa, very few people want to collect paintings done by the Impressionists."

"That is true," the Duke agreed, "but one day, I do not mind betting you, Simonetta, people like Monet, Renoir, and Cézanne will come into their own."

"One day?" Simonetta repeated. "You mean—after they are dead!"

"I am afraid that may be the answer," the Duke replied. "It is a pity that a man has to die before he is appreciated."

"It is very sad, Papa, but I know it is often true," Simonetta agreed. "I appreciate your paintings now, and I hope one day people will appreciate mine."

"I do not mind their appreciating your paintings," the Duke said, "but they can damned well keep their hands off you, or I will take you back to England!"

"Not before I have painted the rocks of Les Baux a dozen times!" Simonetta cried. "Besides, I expect the *Comte* behaves like that with every woman he meets."

"I am sure he does!" the Duke said drily. "But I am not going to let you be counted as one of his 'successes.'"

He spoke so aggressively that Simonetta laughed.

"Forget him, Papa, and let me see what you have been doing this afternoon."

"I have only just started," the Duke replied. "The

light here is so fantastic that there are just not enough colours in my paint-box to put it all onto canvass."

Nevertheless, when he had shown Simonetta what he had painted, she knew that with the light there was at the moment he had somehow managed to depict what he felt rather than saw, and one could feel it in the brilliant colours he had used.

"It is clever, very clever, Papa!" she enthused. "I have a feeling it is going to be a much better painting than anything you have ever done before."

"I hope so," the Duke said. "One is always optimistic about every painting one does until it is finished, and then one knows how much it has fallen short."

"I am sure your friend Claude Monet would be delighted with your progress," Simonetta said with a smile.

They talked about painting until there were noises coming from the kitchen which told them that Marie had arrived back.

"We will have an early meal," the Duke said, "and while you go to bed I am going to walk up to the Inn to see who is staying here."

"If I were not with you, you would have been there before now," Simonetta said with a smile.

"I am not going there for the company," the Duke replied, "but I intend to buy some wine. Not that I expect to entertain, but we should have something in the house to offer any unexpected guests."

"Yes, of course, Papa," Simonetta agreed, "and also to drink ourselves. I have heard about the wines of Provence and how good they are, and it would be a pity not to enjoy them while we are here."

The Duke smiled.

"I have every intention of enjoying the *Château Neuf du Pape*," he said, "which is the most celebrated wine of the Rhône area. I think too we might be extravagant and have an occasional bottle of Champagne."

Simonetta looked at her father.

He was really beginning to enjoy this visit. At the same time, she was afraid that something might upset him and he would take her away and insist on her returning to England.

She might never again have an opportunity to be alone with her father with no-one else to interfere, and she felt she must make the very most of it.

She talked to him gaily all through the meal with which Marie had provided them, and which was delicious.

The chicken cooked in tarragon had a sauce that made Simonetta understand why *Monsieur* Gautier kissed his fingers after eating it.

To start there was a fish dish of red mullet, and to finish there was a soufflé flavoured with a liqueur obviously made from strawberries.

"You are quite right, Marie," the Duke said as she came in to collect the dishes. "You are the best cook not only in Les Baux but in the whole of Provence!"

Marie was clearly pleased at the compliment.

"*Merci, Monsieur*," she said. "I can cook when I have the right ingredients, but that of course means spending money."

"When you have spent all I have given you," the Duke said, "you must come and ask me for more. In the meantime, if *Mademoiselle* and I grow too fat from the way you feed us, we can always blame you."

"You will not be fat, *Monsieur*," Marie said sharply, "you will be well and happy. Which is more than I can say for those 'bags of bones' who come here and paint pictures which are never sold."

She went back to the kitchen without waiting for an answer, and the Duke laughed.

"It is quite obvious," he said, "that the artistic temperament is not appreciated in Les Baux."

"Well, at least they cannot charge for the light!" Simonetta observed.

"I am sure they would if they thought they could get

away with it," the Duke replied. "The French are very quick to grasp at every means of making money."

He rose to his feet as he spoke.

"Go to bed now, Simonetta, and we will both be up early to start working."

"Tomorrow I will go with you," Simonetta replied. "I shall have plenty of time to finish my own painting of the garden when you have other things to do."

"Very well," the Duke smiled, "but I warn you, if you paint that particular view better than I do, I shall be extremely jealous!"

Simonetta kissed his cheek.

"I love you, Papa," she said, "but do not become so engrossed with your artistic friends that you forget I am here."

"I am not likely to do that."

As the Duke spoke he walked away, looking, Simonetta thought, extremely distinguished despite the unconventional and rather shabby clothes he wore.

Marie had already cleared the table and was noisily washing up the dishes in the kitchen.

Simonetta went to the door of the house.

The sun was sinking in a blaze of glory.

Already overhead the sky was darkening and she knew that soon the stars would come out over Les Baux.

'I hope there will be a moon,' she thought to herself.

Many of the books she had read had said there was nothing more beautiful or more mysterious than the moonlight over the great stones and the ruined Castle.

She suddenly decided that she was not tired, despite the fact that it had been a long day.

She walked out into the garden and onto the dusty road along which her father had gone and which at the end climbed gradually up to the heights of Les Baux itself.

"I must see the ruins of the Castle and think of the glory of the days when there was a Court there and

Troubadours sang of a love that was idealistic and pure," she told herself.

Wondering what it had been like in those days, Simonetta walked a little way along the road until on the left-hand side she saw what appeared to be a beautifully carved stone monument.

It had captured the last light of the sun, and while the interior was in shadow, its domed roof seemed to glow as if it were decorated with precious stones.

Curious to find out what it was, Simonetta walked on towards it and climbed over a little hedge of wild lavender.

When she reached it she found that despite the fact that it must be very old it was in good condition, and inside there were pillars to support the domed roof and what appeared to be seats on which one could sit.

She walked inside, and as she did so she had the feeling, perhaps because it was old, that those who had used it had left behind an impression of themselves and she felt almost as if they were speaking to her.

She sat for a moment on the cool stones.

Then she went back to the doorway to stand with her hands outstretched on the pillars on each side of it, and looked up to where towering high against the darkening sky was one of the flat stones of Les Baux, the light from the sun illuminating it vividly and with an almost uncanny radiance.

She felt as if the brilliance of it was somehow absorbed within herself and she too reflected the light.

Then as if she knew she had to return she dropped her head to look down, when she heard a voice say:

"Do not move! Stay just as you are!"

It was an order so sharp, so unexpected, that she froze into immobility and at the same time stared towards where the sound had come from.

Then she was aware that amongst the shrubs and bushes directly in front of her was the shadowy figure of a man. He was sitting in the shadows with an easel in front of him, and it was obvious that he was painting the building in which she was standing.

Simonetta smiled and knew that she had inadvertently stepped into an artist's painting, and nothing would be more disappointing for him than that she should move when he had added her to his composition.

"Raise your head and look up as you were just now!" he ordered.

Amused by the fact that he had not requested her to do so more politely, she raised her face and looked towards the light that was now fading from the rock.

She stood quite still for some minutes in silence. Then he exclaimed:

"*Mon Dieu!* Can anything be more infuriating than that the light has gone? Now I can no longer see you."

As he spoke the artist rose from where he was sitting and walked across the uncut grass towards Simonetta.

She waited for him to come, wondering what he would look like.

She knew from the way he had spoken that his voice was cultured and educated.

As he drew nearer she saw that he was tall, younger than she had somehow expected, and had dark hair.

He stood in front of her, then he said:

"I thought you must be Queen Joanna herself!"

"Who was she?" Simonetta enquired.

"This was her Temple," he replied, "and she was, of course, one of the Queens of the Court of Love."

"How fascinating!" Simonetta exclaimed. "I thought that anything to do with the Court would be inside the Castle."

Although it was hard to see, she thought that the man facing her smiled.

"The followers of the Queen had this little Temple erected for her outside the Castle so that she could visit it when she wished, and of course locally the *jeunes filles* come here to pray that they will find a man who will love them passionately!"

He paused before he added:

"Is that what you were doing?"

"Nothing so romantic," Simonetta replied, laughing. "I was merely exploring."

"By yourself, at this hour? Or are you looking for adventure?"

"I was just looking round."

"Then I am very grateful for whatever inspired you to do so," the artist said. "You were exactly what I wanted for the centre of my painting."

"You are painting very late."

"I have been painting all day. It would not come right, then suddenly you were there," the artist said, "and I knew you were just what was needed to make my painting perfect."

Simonetta laughed again.

"If that is so, *Monsieur*, then I am certainly glad that I have been able to help you."

She stepped down from the Temple and started to move away when he exclaimed:

"Not so fast! Where are you going?"

"Back to where I came from."

"But you cannot!"

"Why not?"

"Because you could not be so cruel, so insensitive, as not to allow me to finish my painting of you, and that means that you must pose here again for me tomorrow."

Simonetta shook her head.

I cannot do that. I shall be busy painting myself."

"You are an artist?"

"I try to be."

"You look too young and certainly too beautiful to worry about art, except where it concerns your appearance."

"I do not think so," Simonetta replied, "and so, *Monsieur*, good-night and *bonne chance!*"

"If you leave me like this," the artist said, "I swear I will have everyone in Les Baux out looking for you, and

I shall certainly follow you to wherever you are going."

Simonetta turned round to look up at him.

His face was in shadow, yet she had the feeling that she could trust him and he was not just making a fuss of her in order to prevent her from leaving. After a moment she said quietly:

"Am I really essential to the completion of your painting?"

"It will never be completed without you."

"How long will it take you to paint me?"

"Not very long. It was just that when you stood in the Temple with your arms outstretched, the whole composition came to life. Before that it had been dead, and I knew there was something wrong. Now I know that what it lacked was you!"

What he said was not pretentious, nor was there an ingratiating note in his voice. Instead, it was as if he was stating a simple fact and speaking the truth.

Simonetta smiled.

"Very well," she said. "I will come back tomorrow, but perhaps a little earlier than this evening!"

"Why not in the morning?" the artist asked.

"Because I am going to be painting with my . . ."

Simonetta checked herself before she said the word "father," then substituted "Master."

"Who is he? Somebody whose name I should know?" the artist enquired.

"I doubt it," Simonetta replied, "because he is English."

"I knew that while your French is exceptional, *Mademoiselle*, and one might almost say Parisian, there was something about you that did not ring true. Now may I compliment you on speaking my language almost perfectly!"

"*Merci, Monsieur,* that is a compliment which I . . . appreciate."

The last light of the sun flickered and died, and now they were talking to each other completely in shadow.

"Tomorrow I will be able to see you," the artist said. "And even if I never finish it my painting will always remain in my head."

"Like 'An Unfinished Symphony,'" Simonetta said without thinking.

"And equally to be regretted," the artist replied, "so let us hope it does not happen."

"I have already promised you that I will sit . . . or perhaps 'stand' is the right word . . . for you again."

"I am endeavouring to believe that you will help me and not vanish like Queen Joanna into the mists of the past, and that you are real and not a ghost."

"I hope not," Simonetta said. "I am always so sorry for ghosts. I have a feeling that they haunt places not because they wish to frighten or distress those who see them, but because they are looking for the happiness that they have lost."

"Perhaps that is why Les Baux is full of ghosts," the artist suggested. "Perhaps those from the Court of Love, having lost the love that meant so much to them, are still looking for it all through the centuries."

"That is too sad!" Simonetta exclaimed. "And if one knew . . . real love, I think one would be . . . grateful even if one could not . . . keep it for . . . ever."

There was silence. Then the artist said:

"You talk as if you have never been in love."

As if she realised that she was being far too conversational and intimate with a stranger, Simonetta said quickly:

"I . . . I must go now . . . *bonsoir, Monsieur.* I will come . . . again tomorrow."

"You must allow me to escort you back to where you are staying," the artist answered. "I am not thrusting myself upon you, but merely taking a precaution for your safety."

"I cannot believe that I am in any danger in Les Baux."

"There are always dangers for a beautiful woman who

walks alone, especially in a place that is redolent with love both of the past and of the present."

"I think I shall be . . . quite safe," Simonetta said. "I have only a very . . . short way to go."

She walked away from him as she spoke, but without saying any more the artist followed her.

Only when they came to the hedge of lavender and she paused, thinking she might stumble in the darkness, did he put out his hand, and without really thinking about it she gave him hers.

The grasp of his fingers was strong and she had the strange feeling that there was a vibration coming from them. Then she was sure that it was just part of her imagination.

He helped her over the hedge and they walked along the dusty roadway.

"Have you far to go?" the artist asked as she took her hand from his.

"I really live . . . next door."

"Then you are in Gautier's house?"

"Yes, he has lent it to my Master. You know him?"

"Very well by reputation. I would let him handle my paintings if I wished to sell them."

Simonetta smiled, remembering that that was what her father had said to the *Comte*.

It was too dark to see, but as if he knew instinctively he asked:

"Why are you smiling?"

Simonetta told him the truth.

"You have made me . . . aware that you are not as . . . desperate for money as so many of the other artists are . . . at least the Impressionists."

"And an Impressionist is what I try to be."

"That is what I want to be too," she said, "and where could be a better place to practise than in Les Baux?"

"That is exactly what I think."

"Do you . . . come here often?"

"As often as I can."

She thought that perhaps he found it expensive, and she asked:

"Where do you live? In Paris?"

"As it happens, I come from Normandy."

"So that is why you are so tall for a Frenchman!"

As she spoke she thought again that it was perhaps a somewhat intimate thing to say, and she was glad it was too dark for him to see the blush that rose in her cheeks.

"So you noticed my height," he said quietly.

"You were . . . walking against the last light from the . . . sun as you came . . . towards me."

"And you were facing it. So there was just enough light for me to see how beautiful you are!"

Simonetta stiffened.

She supposed he was flirting with her, and she knew how angry it would make her father if he knew.

By this time they had reached the gate which led into the garden of Gautier's house.

She turned and put out her hand.

"We are here, *Monsieur!*" she said. "Thank you for . . . escorting me . . . home."

The artist took her hand. Then he said:

"Forgive me if I offended you by being too frank, but I was of course speaking as a painter."

His words made Simonetta feel that she had been conceited in thinking it had been anything else and that she also behaved in a rather foolish manner.

"I am . . . sorry."

"No, you were quite right," he said. "Beware of flattery, beware of strange men who talk to you in a Temple of Love. I have a feeling, although I may be wrong, that you are very young and this is not something you do frequently."

"That is . . . true."

She had the feeling that she should leave him and go straight into the house and not continue this conversation.

And yet he was holding her hand and somehow it was impossible to pull it away.

"You have promised to see me again," the artist said in a low voice, "but you have not told me your name."

"It is . . . Simonetta!"

"Of course! I might have known!"

Because she felt it might be embarrassing for him to ask any more questions, she asked:

"And yours . . . *Monsieur?*"

"Pierre Valéry."

"And you are a well-known painter?"

He shook his head.

"I wish I could answer that question in the affirmative, but I have to tell you that no-one has heard of me. Not yet!"

"But you think and . . . hope that they . . . will?"

"Shall I say there is no Impressionist who does not wish to achieve fame, not only for himself but for the creed he is trying to convey, a creed for those who are prepared to listen."

"It is . . . difficult when you know you have . . . something to give the world which, once it is . . . understood, will help and illumine those who need . . . inspiration."

Simonetta spoke in the same way she would have spoken to her father and the words came from her heart.

There was a little silence. Then Pierre Valéry asked:

"How can you understand, when you are so young and at the same time so exquisitely lovely? Thank you for what you have just said!"

There was no doubt of the sincerity in his voice.

Simonetta felt moved in a way which she could not explain, but it seemed to pulsate through her, and once again she was very conscious of the vibrations from the artist's fingers as he held hers.

"Good-night . . . *Monsieur!*" she said in a voice that was barely above a whisper.

Then she was running quickly into the safety of the small, red-roofed house.

Chapter Three

Simonetta pushed back her hair from her forehead because she was feeling hot.

The sun was beating down as her eyes took in the iridescent light that seemed to reflect and rereflect everywhere she looked.

She stared at her canvass and thought despairingly that she would never capture the radiance and luminosity of Les Baux and she might as well give up the attempt.

Then she told herself that she should not be fainthearted, and she wondered what her father was feeling.

She looked to where he was painting a little way from her.

She had deliberately chosen a different view of the towering white rocks from the ones he had started to portray yesterday.

It was a challenge to any artist to try to put down on canvass the rocks themselves, bare and in some ways menacing.

Beneath them were the flowering trees, the dark cypresses standing like sentinels, and the brilliance of the yellow gorse against the dark purple of the lavender that was just coming into bloom.

"It is all too much at once!" Simonetta told herself,

understanding now why Les Baux was a challenge to every artist who came here!

She knew this morning that her father was a little disappointed by the artists he had met last night.

He was never very conversational at breakfast, but she gathered that he had not enjoyed himself as much as he had thought he would, and she hoped that in consequence he would not blame her for his disappointment.

However, as they finished breakfast he had said:

"I understand that Paul Cézanne will be arriving today, although of course he is always unpredictable."

"I think you said that he lives here in Provence," Simonetta replied.

"He does," the Duke answered. "He has a Studio at Aix on his family property. His friends to whom I was talking last night said that he was coming over to meet me, and they have been expecting him for several days."

The Duke saw the expression on Simonetta's face and said:

"I know you want to meet him, and I will try to bring him here, but I have no wish for you to go to the Inn."

He said no more, but picked up his canvass and easel.

"You are coming with me?" he enquired as he walked towards the door.

"Of course, Papa," Simonetta replied.

Because she felt it was what he wanted, she did not chatter as they walked away from the house and down the dusty lane to the place that the Duke had selected yesterday as the scene for his first painting in Les Baux.

Only when she had found an aspect that she wished to paint herself did she find herself wondering how Pierre Valéry was progressing with his sketch of the Temple of Love.

Simonetta now remembered two things: first, that she had not told her father of her adventure of the night before, and secondly, that she had promised to pose for Pierre Valéry early this evening, forgetting that they were to dine with the *Comte*.

She could tackle the first problem, she told herself, by telling her father about it when they had luncheon.

Then she remembered that he had said that if she became involved in any way with a man he would take her home.

"It is not really that I am involved," she reasoned to herself.

At the same time, he might think it reprehensible that she had left the house after he had expected her to go to bed.

He would also be perturbed that she had conversed with a strange artist to whom she had not been introduced and whom he did not know.

"I had better say nothing," she told herself, "not because I am ... ashamed of what I have done ... but merely because it ... might upset Papa."

She looked at him in the distance, thinking how even when he was sitting at an easel he looked both handsome and distinguished.

However much he tried to disguise himself in artistic and unconventional clothes, he still had about him an authority and a nobility which were quite undisguisable.

She wondered whether the same applied to her, but she thought it was unlikely that anybody meeting her would think she was an aristocrat incognito.

She was sensible enough to realise that from her father's point of view this would make her even more vulnerable than she was already.

'I must not upset him at the start of our adventure together,' she thought, 'otherwise he will never bring me again.'

This morning she had dressed herself without the assistance of a lady's-maid, and Marie had just placed the food down on the breakfast-table, leaving them to help themselves.

She could understand how her father felt at being able to get away occasionally from the pomp and circumstance that existed at Faringham Park and his other houses.

As he had said, he was always looked after, cosseted, and fussed over, and the same applied to her.

When she was small there had been a Nanny and a nursemaid who attended her, besides a housemaid and a footman whose duties were to wait on the Nursery.

Later there had been Governesses, not one but a number who were experts in the subjects which her father considered important for her education.

Unlike the majority of noble families, who educated their sons and neglected their daughters, the Duke was insistent that Simonetta should have the same chance as her brothers had been given to develop her intellect.

Therefore, besides the resident Governesses and of course Nanny, who had remained with her until her retirement, there were French, Greek, and Latin teachers, Music Masters, and various other instructors on any subjects that Simonetta wished to be taught.

She had even been coached in mathematics, which she had found extremely boring and with the result that even now she had difficulty in doing complicated sums.

Having so many people to serve her made her feel that she was confined and restricted, and now for the first time in her life she was, like her father, free.

It would therefore be very stupid, she thought to herself, to make him feel apprehensive by admitting that after he had left her she was getting into mischief.

"He would certainly not like me to talk to Pierre Valéry," she decided.

She was quite certain that her father would forbid her to see him again and would make her promise that when he left the house she would not go out without him.

"I will just forget to tell him what happened," Simonetta said to herself, looking up at the blue sky.

She thought the sunshine somehow exonerated her from any sense of sin.

The other problem was more difficult.

Because she had made a promise and because she thought it would be exceedingly rude to ignore Pierre Valéry's compliment of wanting her in his painting, she knew she must tell him that she had forgotten a previous engagement.

Not to turn up would not only be rude, but she had the feeling that he would be disappointed.

"It is because I am essential to the composition of his painting," Simonetta argued to herself.

But she knew, if she was honest, that she had the instinctive feeling that he wanted to see her for herself, and it was what she herself wanted also.

An emptiness inside told her that it was time for luncheon, and even as she thought of it she saw her father waving to her.

"We must go back now," he said.

Simonetta picked up her canvass, folded her easel, and started to walk through the long grass towards where her father had been working.

"How have you got on, my dearest?" her father asked as she reached him.

"Not very well," Simonetta admitted. "The trouble is that it is too beautiful and in a way too overwhelming for me. I think I will do better with something smaller and easier."

The Duke laughed.

"That is certainly being chicken-hearted."

"I know," Simonetta said, "but you must agree it is more difficult than anything we have ever tried to paint before."

"That is true," her father replied, "but we have to go on trying, not only with painting but with everything else in life."

She smiled at him.

He picked up his canvass and easel and without saying any more started to walk in the direction of the house.

Although she wanted to see the result of his work, she knew that it annoyed her father to have to show what he was doing until he was ready to do so.

They walked in silence, both acutely aware of the beauty all round them and with the satisfying feeling that they were hungry and were about to eat a luncheon that would be delicious.

Then as they reached the house Simonetta found the answer to what was worrying her.

After luncheon she would make some excuse for her father to go ahead, and then she would walk to where she had met Pierre Valéry the night before.

He might want to put her in the centre of his canvass, but he would have plenty to do on the rest of the painting until she was ready to pose for him.

The luncheon was as good as they had expected it to be, and Simonetta chatted to her father, making him laugh so that the time passed quickly, and only when he had finished his second cup of coffee did the Duke say:

"We must not waste the sunlight. What makes everything so difficult is that the pattern of light changes with every hour, almost every minute, and I keep altering what I have already done, so that at this rate I shall never finish a painting!"

"Of course you will, Papa!" Simonetta replied. "You must do at least two or three so that we can take them home to remind us whenever we feel depressed how lovely and exciting everything was here."

The Duke put his hand on her head as he rose from the table.

"You are a good child, Simonetta," he said. "I like having you with me. You were quite right: I would have been lonely if I had been by myself."

"And I adore being with you, Papa."

The Duke picked up his canvass.

"Are you ready?" he asked.

"You go ahead, Papa. I will join you," Simonetta replied. "I want to find a hat to wear, otherwise I may have sunstroke. There is no reason for you to wait for me."

"No, of course not, I will go on," the Duke replied.

As soon as he had gone, Simonetta went upstairs to her bedroom, finding a large, shady hat that she had put on top of her trunk at the last minute.

It was made of a soft straw which would not crush, and now she thought she would be glad of it in the heat of the afternoon sun.

When she was ready she went downstairs to put everything else she required ready to pick up on her way back after seeing Pierre Valéry.

Then she walked along the road towards the Temple, aware that her father had already disappeared in the opposite direction.

Simonetta moved quickly and as she went she wondered what she would do if Pierre Valéry was not there.

It would be difficult to see him later in the day without her father being aware of it.

She had the idea that it might take some time to reach the *Comte*'s *Château*, in which case he would send the horses early in the evening for them.

She suspected that he would have told her father the exact time, but the Duke had either forgotten or had not bothered to tell her what it was.

Anyway, she knew that she must come back earlier so as to wash and to change her gown before they left, even though she had nothing very suitable in which to go out in the evening.

She had reached the edge of the rough land in which the Temple lay, and she could see the hedge of lavender ahead before she was able to look through the trees to where Pierre Valéry had sat the day before.

For one moment she thought he was not there. Then

she saw him and felt her heart give a leap of relief.

She had climbed over the hedge and was walking towards him before he saw her.

Then he looked up and she thought at first there was an expression of incredulity on his face before he rose to his feet.

He was standing with his palette in his hand when she reached him, and now she could see his face clearly for the first time and thought he was even more handsome than he had appeared in the semi-darkness.

His antecedents certainly showed in the fairness of his skin, but his eyes were not the bright blue that many Normandy people possessed, but were dark.

There was no doubt of his delight at seeing her, because there was a smile of welcome on his firm, chiselled lips.

Because Simonetta had hurried through the long grass she was breathless by the time she reached him.

"I am honoured that you have come," he said, "and at the same time I am relieved to find that you are real. I have been convincing myself all night that you were a ghost or an apparition from the past and I would never see you again."

Because he was speaking in the same quiet tone of voice as he had the previous evening, Simonetta felt that he was not paying her an extravagant compliment but was stating a fact.

She laughed.

"I am real . . . and I am here! But only to tell you that I cannot keep my promise to . . . model for you this . . . evening."

"Why not?"

The question was sharp.

"Because I completely forgot that my . . . Master and I have promised to dine out tonight."

Pierre Valéry raised his eye-brows.

"I did not realise there was anybody in Les Baux who was in the habit of giving dinner-parties."

"We are not dining in Les Baux."

"Is it impertinent of me to enquire where?"

"There is no secret about it," Simonetta replied. "The *Comte* Jacques de Laval, who is a collector of paintings by Impressionists, has asked us to his *Château*."

"The *Comte!*" Pierre Valéry murmured almost beneath his breath.

"You know him?"

"I have heard of him."

"He bought *Summer* by Monet, which is a painting I want to see, and he says he has in his collection many other paintings which he has bought from *Monsieur* Gautier, in whose house we are staying."

"And of course the dinner-party at the *Château* of the *Comte* is much more important than modelling for my poor composition."

He spoke rather disagreeably and Simonetta said quickly:

"Forgive me! I am sorry to let you down, but I really did forget the dinner, and I . . . naturally have to go with my . . . Master."

"You mean he would think it very strange if you wished to stay behind?" Pierre Valéry asked.

"Very strange indeed," Simonetta agreed.

There was silence. Then Pierre Valéry said:

"As you are here, will you not stand in the Temple as you did last night, and at least I can get a little further with the outline of your figure than I have done already."

Simonetta hesitated.

Unconsciously she looked over her shoulder in the direction her father had gone.

It must have been the expression on her face or the gesture which made Pierre Valéry say:

"I think you have not yet told your Master, as you call him, that you have met me."

Simonetta started and a blush came to her cheeks.

At first she thought she would say: "Of course I

have!" Then an honesty that was characteristic of her made her say:

"No . . . as a matter of fact I did not . . . mention . . . you."

"Why not?"

"I . . . I thought it would be . . . a mistake . . . ."

Although she felt there was no reason why she should answer his questions, she nevertheless felt compelled to do so.

"When my Master left me last night to go to the Inn, I . . . told him I was . . . going to . . . bed."

"Would he think it so strange that you should change your mind?"

"He would think it a . . . mistake for me to talk to . . . somebody to whom I have not been . . . introduced."

As she spoke she realised that Pierre Valéry raised his eye-brows and looked definitely surprised.

"Surely," he asked, "as you are on your own, so to speak, you are entitled to live your own life when you are not being instructed?"

There was a definite pause while Simonetta sought for an answer.

"I think," she said slowly, "that my . . . Master feels he is . . . responsible for me."

Pierre Valéry smiled.

"That is very sensible, and may I say that I do not appreciate the modern young woman who thinks she can be independent and look after herself."

"That is what I . . . think I can . . . do," Simonetta said firmly.

"It is certainly something you should not do."

"Why? Why . . . should you . . . think that?"

He smiled again before he said:

"Because anyone who is as beautiful as you are needs to be protected and certainly kept safe from wolves—invariably in sheep's clothing—who are always looking out for somebody just like you."

Simonetta laughed.

"You make it sound very exciting, but I have not seen any wolves so far. If I did, I would . . . recognise them."

"Do not be too sure of that."

"I think I should know if somebody was . . . wicked or . . . sinful," Simonetta said.

She was arguing in the same way as she argued with her father, not only for the fun of it but also because it made her express her ideas, which invariably inspired new ones.

"So, you are perceptive," Pierre Valéry said.

"I hope so. My instinct is very acute, and I am even aware of the . . . vibrations of those who lived here in the Castle and those who fought against it. They have become part of the beauty here and are inescapable."

She spoke dreamily, feeling as if the words came into her mind almost as if they were being placed there.

"I understand what you are saying," Pierre Valéry said, "since I feel the same."

"Of course you do," Simonetta replied. "Impressionists train themselves to feel rather than to see, to reach out and sense that which is hidden to more ordinary, mundane people."

"That is what we wish to believe we are like," Pierre Valéry said, "although for some it may be just a pretence, and not intuitively true, as it is for you."

Because she was pleased at what he had said about her, Simonetta smiled at him and as she did so her eyes met his, and it was difficult to look away.

"I . . . I must . . . go."

She spoke with her mind and was afraid to listen to her heart.

"Not before you have posed for me," Pierre Valéry said. "If it will make it easier, I will speak to your Master and ask him if he will permit you to help me."

"No, no! You must not do that!" Simonetta said quickly. "As I have already told you . . . he will be . . . annoyed that we have met so . . . unconventionally."

Pierre Valéry looked puzzled.

"I do not understand," he said. "Surely as an Art Student, and as your parents allow you to go abroad with your teacher, you are living what to most girls of your age would seem a very free and unconventional manner."

"Yes, of course I am," Simonetta agreed quickly, "but I would not wish my Master to be angry because I am wasting my time talking as so many painters do, when he wants me to paint."

"So you know that is a very prevailing habit of our kind," Pierre Valéry said with a smile.

"Yes, of course I know that," Simonetta said, because she felt that he expected it of her.

Once again he looked at her strangely and said:

"As you are free to do anything you like, I beg you not to spoil my painting by not coming back. Your relationship with your Master does not concern me one way or another unless it prevents you from helping me to finish what I am certain will be hailed in the Salons as 'The Picture of the Year.'"

As they were both aware that for an Impressionist this could never happen, Simonetta knew he was being sarcastic and laughed.

"I will stay for just five minutes," she said, "and perhaps tomorrow when my Master goes to the Inn I shall be able to come here again as I did yesterday evening."

"For the best results," Pierre Valéry said, "you must come as early as you can, before the light goes."

"It would be more romantic if you painted the Temple of Love by moonlight."

"I have already thought of that," he replied, "but there are other places in Les Baux that are more sensational when the moon is bright. Have you seen them?"

Simonetta shook her head.

"You know I only arrived yesterday."

Pierre Valéry smiled.

"Then that is something really wonderful for you to look forward to. Will you promised me something?"

"I'm afraid of making promises I may not be able to keep. I always try to keep my promises, and I think it is . . . dishonest to break one's . . . word."

"I agree with you," Pierre Valéry answered, "and therefore I want you to promise me, *Mademoiselle* Simonetta, that you will let me be the first person to show you Les Baux by moonlight."

Simonetta's eyes lit up.

"Would you do that?" she asked. "It is something I want to see very much, but with somebody who knows the best places. Otherwise I may miss the most beautiful ones."

"I promise you that with me to guide you, you will miss nothing," Pierre Valéry said.

Simonetta thought. Then she said:

"It will be . . . difficult."

"I will wait."

It flashed through her mind that her father would be furious if he knew.

At the same time, he had said nothing about taking her to see Les Baux by moonlight, and she had the feeling that tomorrow night he would want to go to the Inn, especially if Cézanne was there.

Because her conscience pricked her, she thought that perhaps before then she would be able to mention casually that she had met Pierre Valéry.

Even then her father would think it strange, and perhaps reprehensible, that she had met a man when she should have been inside the house.

"I will be waiting tomorrow night," Pierre Valéry said quietly.

"If it is possible, I will come."

As she spoke she thought she was making a decision that in some way might have dire consequences.

It was almost as if she threw a stone into a pond of

still water and knew that from the point of impact the ripples would not cease until they reached the sides.

Then she told herself that she was being imaginative.

Her instinct told her that she could trust Pierre Valéry, although she had no idea why she knew it.

She wanted so much to see Les Baux in the moonlight, and she was absolutely certain that Pierre Valéry would do nothing that would upset or distress her.

'He is an artist, and I am trying to be one,' she thought. 'That is the bond we have in common. Besides, he would think it very strange and out of character if I insisted on having a Chaperone.'

It was something her father would expect her to have if she was alone with any man, but for Lady Simonetta Terrington-Trench it would be outrageous to be friendly with an artist whose associates had been vilified, attacked, and denounced not only for their ideals but for their behaviour.

Simonetta knew that her father's friends in England and their relations would be horrified at the idea of her even speaking to such a person.

"I might as well enjoy myself while I have the chance," she told her defiantly.

She also knew that once she was back in England and presented at Court, she would be strictly chaperoned by day and by night and her father had already chosen those of her relatives who would undertake the task.

"A chance like this will never come again."

The words seemed to be whispered in her mind, and she thought perhaps the stones of Les Baux themselves were laughing at her for being prudish and reluctant to enjoy her independence while she had it.

"I will come . . . I promise I will . . . come," she said aloud, and saw by the light that came into Pierre Valéry's eyes that he was pleased.

"Now I will pose for just five minutes," she went on,

"otherwise my Master will wonder what has happened to me."

She did not wait for him to agree but ran away across the rough grass towards the Temple.

She reached it and walked inside to stand as she had the night before, with her arms oustretched and her head thrown back as she looked up at the towering rocks overhead.

She was wearing a white gown and her body seemed to blend with the ancient carved stone, and only her hair flared like a flame, a vivid patch of colour which appeared to be dancing in the light of the sun.

Pierre Valéry stared at the picture she made and knew that even Botticelli himself would have found it difficult to capture the mystic beauty of it on canvass.

He stood looking at her for a long moment. Then he frantically began to paint.

* * *

Simonetta saw that her father was still engrossed in his painting, but now that the shadows had deepened and changed colour and the sun was lower in the Heavens, she picked up her canvass.

She was not very satisfied with what she had done and she thought that tomorrow she would start again. Perhaps then her hand would feel as if it were guided from above to save her from making more of a mess with every stroke of her brush.

She walked towards her father, who was concentrating so deeply on his work that he did not know she was there until she spoke.

"I think I should return to the house now, Papa."

"Already?" he questioned.

"It is growing late, and if we are to dine with the *Comte* I must change and make myself look a little less scruffy than I do at the moment."

The Duke smiled.

"I have never seen you look that," he said, "but I suppose we must tidy ourselves even though by our appearance we will hardly grace the elegant *Château*, which I suspect the *Comte* owns."

"Do you know anything about him except that he patronises the Impressionists?" Simonetta enquired.

"Very little," the Duke replied, "except that like all rich Frenchmen he lives in great luxury, but not, I imagine, in the style of the Lords of Les Baux!"

Simonetta laughed.

"Instead of dining with the *Comte*," she said, "I wish we could be dining in the Castle as it was in the past. Think how exciting that would be!"

"It would indeed," the Duke agreed, "but there would be no painting by Monet to admire, which is in fact our only excuse for wasting our time, which is so precious."

The way her father spoke made Simonetta look at him sharply.

"I am glad you do not like the *Comte*, Papa," she remarked, "because I do not like him either."

The Duke did not reply but looked down at his painting until after a moment Simonetta asked:

"Must we dine with him tonight?"

"It would certainly be rude to cancel now, having accepted his invitation," the Duke answered, "but quite frankly, Simonetta, he is a type for whom I have no use. When we have seen his paintings we will not concern ourselves with him again."

Simonetta knew without her father telling her that he was annoyed by the compliments the *Comte* had paid her and the way he had kissed her hand.

"You are very wise, Papa," she said, "and of course I agree with you."

Without waiting for the Duke to answer, she started to walk back to the house.

When she reached it she found that Marie had

prepared a hip-bath for her in the small *toilette* which opened out of her father's bedroom.

It was the way Louis Gautier bathed when he was in residence, and there were two cans of water ready for Simonetta to pour into the bath, one still very hot, the other one cold.

After she had her bath she ran upstairs to try to decide what she should wear.

There was not a great choice. She had no evening-gowns amongst her luggage, and she therefore chose a pink afternoon one which she had worn when she was younger.

Mrs. Baines had altered it by sweeping the full skirt round the back in imitation of a small bustle and had added a sash with a large bow.

It certainly did not look as if it came from Frederick Worth, but it was very pretty for a young girl and had obviously not cost a great deal of money.

On her father's instructions, since she came abroad with him Simonetta had worn her long hair coiled into a tight chignon at the back of her head.

Now she arranged it more fashionably, at the same time being careful not to do it in the elaborate manner which her lady's-maid at home had perfected so as to be ready for her début in London.

"I do not want to look like the beggar-maid at the feast," Simonetta said to herself. "At the same time, the *Comte* himself must not be suspicious that I am anything other than what I appear to be."

She was too innocent to be aware that for the *Comte* to think she was an Art Student was very much more dangerous than if he suspected she was in fact a Lady of Quality.

The Duke, lingering over his painting, was not ready when the carriage arrived.

But Simonetta was downstairs when the footman knocked, wearing a somewhat pretentious livery and looking, she thought with amusement, somewhat disdainful at having to call at so small and insignificant a house.

She went to the door of her father's bedroom.

"The carriage is here, Papa!"

"Let it wait," the Duke replied. "I cannot find my collar-stud."

Simonetta went into the room and found what he was seeking in a neat little box provided by Jarvis which had not only about a dozen collar-studs in it but also several pairs of cuff-links.

"How could I know where he had hidden it?" the Duke asked in an irritated tone. "I have a good mind to go out to dinner without a tie and be comfortable."

"You should, Papa."

"I wish I had never accepted this damned-fool invitation."

He fastened his collar-stud and added:

"It was a great mistake, Simonetta, and one should never be made to mix in higher social circles when one is comfortably at ease with outcasts!"

"Who are undoubtedly far more amusing!" Simonetta laughed.

"I will go to the Inn," the Duke said. "Go tell the carriage we are not coming."

Simonetta gave a little cry.

"You cannot do that, Papa! It would really be too rude, and perhaps it would make the *Comte* take a dislike to all Impressionists and never buy any of their paintings again."

"That is certainly a thought," her father agreed, "and as there are few of them who are not in desperate need of selling a painting to keep themselves alive, I suppose I must sacrifice myself."

"And we must certainly persuade the *Comte* to enlarge his collection of modern art," Simonetta said.

The Duke put on a velvet coat which Simonetta laughingly called one of his "props" when he went on one of his secret trips.

"Come on, Simonetta," he said, "if we have to be bored we had better get it over as quickly as possible."

As he spoke he looked at his daughter for the first time.

"Why are you dressed up like that?" he asked sharply.

"Dressed up, Papa?"

"Where are the gowns that you altered especially for this trip?"

"This is one of them."

"Well, you look too smart in it," the Duke said crossly. "No flirting with the *Comte*, and we leave as soon after dinner as is possible."

"Yes, of course, Papa. That suits me, and all I want, like you, is to see his paintings."

The frown faded from between the Duke's eyes.

"We should never have become involved with the chap," he said, "and we will come home as soon as we have seen the paintings."

The carriage waiting for them outside was closed but the Duke asked for it to be opened.

Simonetta found it fascinating to drive by the light of the setting sun up through the rocks to the Castle of Les Baux and then down into the valley on the other side.

The view as they did so was breathtaking.

Then they were moving along the roads where the branches of the trees met overhead to make a tunnel of dark shade.

They passed through several small villages that were beautiful in themselves, their streets bordered with trees and at the end of them arches or monuments erected in Roman times.

The journey took half-an-hour until they crossed a bridge and saw, situated amongst the trees, the towers and roofs of the *Château*.

It looked very impressive in the distance and even more so as they drew closer to it.

As they drove up the drive, Simonetta could not help

feeling thrilled that she would have the chance while she was in France to see the inside of a private *Château*.

She had read about them and her father had told her how attractive they were, but it was one thing to imagine what a *Château* would be like and another to actually visit one.

They were escorted through a Hall in which there was a carved stone staircase curving upwards to a high landing.

Then they were shown into a Salon which Simonetta saw at one glance was as elegant as she had expected, and it was hung with the paintings she and her father both wanted to see.

The *Comte* was waiting for them, very smart in his evening-clothes, and beside him was a very attractive and elegant woman whose gown instantly made Simonetta feel as if she were dressed in rags.

"Welcome, *Monsieur* Calvert!" the *Comte* said genially, advancing towards them. "And welcome, *Mademoiselle* Simonetta! It is a great pleasure to have you here."

They shook hands but he did not kiss Simonetta's, for which she was grateful. Then he said:

"Allow me to present you to my sister, who has arrived unexpectedly. The *Comtesse* de la Tour— *Monsieur* Clyde Calvert and *Mademoiselle* Simonetta!"

The *Comtesse*, who had dark flashing eyes like her brother's, looked at the Duke with what Simonetta thought was such surprise that she felt it was insulting, and barely acknowledged Simonetta's existence.

"*Tiens!*" she exclaimed. "My brother did not tell me that Impressionists had suddenly become tall, handsome, and distinguished! This is certainly something new!"

"You flatter me, *Madame*," the Duke replied.

"But of course, you are English," the *Comtesse* went on, "and that is different!"

Now she spoke in English, and it was obvious that

she had learnt the language well and that her French accent was very attractive.

There was Champagne before dinner, which the *Comte* said was from his own vineyards at Épernay, and then they went into the Dining-Room, which also was hung with paintings by French Masters.

Simonetta realised with amusement that the *Comtesse* was making every effort to attract her father and flattering him with an expertise that she could not help admiring because it was so polished and proficient.

"I want to talk to you, *Mademoiselle*," the *Comte* said as his sister monopolised the Duke.

"You must forgive me if I am inattentive," Simonetta replied, "but I am enjoying seeing the inside of a French *Château* for the first time."

"I daresay it is a change from other places in which you have lived," the *Comte* said. "Do you have a room to yourself in Paris, or do you share an apartment with other students like yourself?"

Simonetta's eyes twinkled.

It seemed that despite the Duke's fears, the *Comte* was convinced that she was a student.

She had heard from her father that numbers of students were to be found hanging about the artists in the cafés where they met in Paris.

They were striving to earn a little extra money by sitting as models in Art Classes or for any painter who would employ them.

But to the Impressionists, because of their insistence on painting out-of-doors, they were not particularly important.

The Duke had explained to Simonetta how the students sometimes clashed with the professional models, who resented their chiselling in and often would fight, scratching and disfiguring one another's faces.

"I am very proud of my *Château*," the *Comte* was saying, "which has been in my family for three centuries."

"It was not damaged in the Revolution?" Simonetta asked.

"There was a little trouble at first, but the worst crimes were committed in Paris."

"You must be very proud of your possessions!"

"I am especially proud to be able to show them to you!"

"Your paintings are most interesting," Simonetta said, "and of course I am longing to see Claude Monet's, who is a friend of my Master."

"I will show it to you," the *Comte* promised, "and I hope that by the end of the evening you will be a *friend* of mine."

He accentuated the word "friend", in a way which Simonetta felt gave it a different meaning, and she said quickly:

"You must tell me what other paintings you have bought recently. I have heard how kind you have been to the Impressionists who have great difficulty in selling their paintings."

"I consider myself a good judge of art," the *Comte* said boastfully, "and I am quite certain that in the future, those who have disparaged the new School of Painting will have to eat their words!"

"I hope so, I very much hope so!" Simonetta said.

Then she added jokingly:

"Perhaps by that time even my paintings will be valuable!"

"You would have no difficulty in selling them now if you trusted me to handle them for you," the *Comte* said in a low voice.

Simonetta thought she should tell him that she was in no need of money, but it was difficult to put such an assertion into words without making it seem strange.

Instead, she continued to talk of Monet, Renoir, and any other Impressionists who came to mind.

She had the idea that the *Comte* was not listening to her but was looking at her face with his dark eyes, watching her and appraising her in a way which made her feel shy.

There was no reason for her to feel afraid.

Her father was there, and after they had seen the painting they would leave. Then, as he had said, there would be no need for them to bother with the *Comte* again.

But it was not as easy as it seemed.

After dinner, in French fashion they all left the Dining-Room together and returned to the Salon.

The *Comte* showed them the paintings that hung on the walls, and at the end of the Salon they saw the one by Claude Monet called *Summer*, which was just as beautiful as the Duke and Simonetta had expected it to be.

He also owned two other paintings by Monet, one by Manet, and another by Sisley which was so lovely that Simonetta thought it must have come from some fantasy-world.

She was staring at it, forgetting where she was for the moment, when she realised that the *Comtesse* had drawn her father away into another room adjoining the Salon.

Although she could see them through the open door and hear their voices, she and the *Comte* had been left behind.

She turned instinctively to follow her father, but the *Comte's* hand went out to catch hold of her wrist.

"I want you to talk to me," he said.

"B-but the paintings in the next room . . . I want to see . . . them."

"There is plenty of time for that later."

Simonetta tried to twist her arm away from him, but he held on to it with a strong grip.

"Please . . . you are . . . hurting me!"

"That is not true," the *Comte* replied, "and I have no wish for you to escape me. You are very lovely, Simonetta, so lovely that I have found it impossible to think of anybody else since I first saw you!"

He spoke so strangely and his voice was so deep with an emotion she did not recognise that she looked up at him in astonishment.

His eyes seemed to be blazing down at her and she suddenly felt frightened.

At the same time, she told herself that she must not panic. Her father was next door and within hearing, and there was nothing the *Comte* could do that would upset her.

Again she tried to take her wrist from his grasp and said:

"I do not . . . like being . . . touched."

"I want to touch you," the *Comte* answered, "and there is something I want to say to you."

"What is it?"

She thought he was behaving very strangely. At the same time, she had no wish to make a scene because she knew it would upset her father.

"Calvert is too old for you," the *Comte* said, "and besides that, he cannot look after you in the same way I could."

Simonetta after one quick glance had deliberately not been looking at the *Comte*, but now she turned to stare at him.

"I would dress you in gowns," the *Comte* went on in a deep voice, "that would make you look even more beautiful than you are now. I would buy you jewels, a carriage, and an apartment in Paris that would be the envy of every other woman. We will leave Les Baux and I will take you directly to Paris."

Simonetta was so astonished that for a moment she could only give a little gasp, and her voice seemed to be lost in her throat.

Then, when she was wondering frantically what she should say, what she should reply to such a horrifying suggestion, she saw with relief that the Duke was coming back into the Salon.

Chapter Four

Driving back to Les Baux, Simonetta felt as if she had escaped from something more menacing and frightening than even the *Comte* himself.

She told herself it was because she was shocked and it was something she had never encountered in her life before, and she did not completely understand what his suggestion really meant.

At the same time, she knew it was wrong and wicked and that Pierre Valéry had been right when he had said there were "wolves in sleep's clothing" that would frighten her.

The moment her father came back to the Salon, she had run towards him to slip her arm through his and say:

"You must show me the paintings yourself, *mon maître*. Otherwise I shall miss the best points, and that, I am sure, would be a mistake."

She was aware that her father looked sharply first at her, then at the *Comte*. But he said nothing and simply drew her back into the room which he had just left.

There he took her from painting to painting, pointing out the special way each artist had depicted the light, or the manner in which his brush-work was characteristic of his style.

He spoke with such an air of authority that even the *Comtesse* could not interrupt.

At the same time, Simonetta was aware that the *Comte*, who had followed them, was watching her with an expression in his eyes that she dreaded.

She was terribly afraid that he might in fact say something so revealing that her father would be aware of what had happened.

Fortunately the *Comte* kept silent, but to Simonetta the time that passed before they could leave seemed to drag on and on, and she felt as if she walked a tight-rope and one slip would be disastrous.

She knew how furious her father would be if he had the slightest idea of what the *Comte* had said to her, and while her first instinct was to confide in him, she knew that if she did so there was every likelihood of his taking her back to England the next day.

"How could Papa have guessed, or I either, that the *Comte* would behave in such a shocking manner on such short acquaintance?" Simonetta asked herself when they had left.

While they were in the *Château*, she could think of nothing but keeping close to her father's side and preventing the *Comte* from saying one word to her which could not be overheard.

"When shall we see you again, *Monsieur?*" the *Comtesse* asked the Duke.

She spoke in a soft, seductive voice which told Simonetta that if the *Comte* was enamoured of her, his sister was certainly attracted to her father.

However, she was used to seeing lovely ladies looking at him in a yearning manner and talking to him in a caressing voice that was both inviting and provocative.

She was quite sure that her father could deal with such women very effectively, but as far as Simonetta was concerned, the *Comte* terrified her.

All she wanted to do was get away from the *Château*

and be alone with her father in the little red brick house which now seemed a haven of security.

At last it was possible for them to say farewell, but while Simonetta said firmly: "Good-bye, *Monsieur le Comte!*" his *"Au revoir!"* had, she thought, a menacing sound which told her he firmly intended to see her again.

As they drove away, the Duke threw himself back in the comfortable carriage and said:

"Well, thank God that is over! At least the paintings were worth seeing!"

Simonetta was still not sure whether she should tell her father what had occurred, then decided it would be a mistake.

There was only an infinitesimal pause before she replied:

"They were magnificent, Papa, and I am delighted to have seen them."

"I think *Summer* is one of the best Monet ever did," the Duke said, as if he was following his own thoughts.

"I had no idea that Sisley painted so beautifully."

"I met him while I was in Paris," the Duke said, "but only for a short while. The next time I go, I must make a point of seeing him again."

They talked about Impressionists all the way back, and because she was forcing herself to concentrate on what was being said rather than on what had happened when she was alone with the *Comte*, Simonetta hardly glanced at the view outside the windows of the now closed carriage.

However, she was aware that the stars were coming out and a young moon was lighting up the sky.

But she did not want to think of anything except what her father was saying, and she slipped her arm through his, as though to hold on to him made her feel safe.

Only when she was back at what now seemed to be home, and the Duke was yawning before he went to his bedroom, did she say a little tentatively:

"There will be no . . . reason for us to . . . see the *Comte* again . . . will there, Papa?"

She asked the question because she wanted to be reassured, and the Duke replied:

"No reason at all! I saw him trying to flirt with you at dinner, which I thought a great impertinence, but I suppose his wretched wife is used to his behaviour."

Simonetta started.

"His . . . wife?" she repeated. "Is the *Comte* . . . married?"

"Of course he is married," the Duke replied. "I vaguely remember that she came from a very rich family, so I imagine that it is with her money that he buys paintings for what he calls 'His Collection.'"

Simonetta's lips tightened.

Now the *Comte's* behaviour seemed even more abhorrent than it had before.

She had not imagined that he would be married. However, if he was, that he should suggest taking her to Paris, paying for her gowns, and giving her jewellery was certainly an insult that in any previous century would have been avenged in blood.

Then she told herself perhaps this was something most Art Students would accept, especially if they were as poor as her father had said they were.

She did not still fully understand what the *Comte* expected from her, but she knew that she disliked his touching her, and if he tried to kiss her, as she suspected he might do if they were alone, it would be a horrible experience.

"I will never see him again," she decided.

But when she was alone in her bedroom she felt almost as if he were menacing her and that it would be difficult for her to escape from him.

"Now I am being imaginative," she said aloud.

But her fear persisted that the *Comte* would not be circumvented easily and that he was so conceited that he would doubtless believe he could win her over.

"There is nothing he can do to me," Simonetta told herself, "As I shall be with Papa."

Then the thought came that if she was not with her father she would be with Pierre Valéry, who would protect her.

From what he had said this morning, it was obvious that he did not like the *Comte* and what he had heard about him.

He was right, absolutely right, Simonetta thought, and she decided that if she could not confide in her father, perhaps she would tell Pierre Valéry what had happened.

As she thought it over, lying in the darkness, she decided it was cheapening and degrading that any man should think, even if she actually had been an Art Student, that she would go to Paris with him and accept expensive presents.

"If I were poor, I would still be respectable, and Art Students cannot all behave badly," she argued to herself.

She remembered Pierre Valéry warning her that it was dangerous for a beautiful woman to walk alone, but that it was dangerous to be with men who thought you beautiful was an idea that had never occurred to Simonetta before.

"Whatever happens, I must not spoil this holiday for Papa," she told herself, "and I certainly must not make him apprehensive of what might happen to me."

She knew that if he felt like that he would never bring her away again!

Simonetta thought how frustrating and upsetting it would be if she had to stay at home, even with her favourite Aunt Harriet, and know that her father was at Les Baux or anywhere else in France without her.

She knew if she thought it over sensibly and quietly that she really had nothing to fear, and her father must never be aware of what had occurred.

When she came down to breakfast it was to find him in a very good mood.

"I feel not only that this is a perfect day for painting," he said, "but that everything will go well. Perhaps it was the good wine we had last night, which was certainly different from what I drank at the Inn, but my head is clear and I feel twenty years younger than I did yesterday."

Simonetta laughed.

"Do not get too young, Papa, or I shall be too old to be your daughter."

The Duke smiled at her.

"You are looking very lovely this morning, my dearest!" he said. "But be careful not to sunburn your skin. I like it white, and as you are well aware, poets, and especially the Troubadours, extolled the beauty of a lady's white skin."

"We must try to learn something about the Troubadours while we are here," Simonetta replied.

"We will," the Duke answered.

But she knew that he was not really interested and was thinking about his painting.

They set off as soon as they had finished breakfast and painted industriously until it was time to return for luncheon.

As they were walking back to the house the Duke said:

"I have been thinking that as you want to meet Paul Cézanne, I will go to the Inn, where I am sure I will find him with his friends, and ask him if he will dine here with us tonight."

"That would be lovely, Papa," Simonetta said dutifully, but her heart sank.

If her father had Cézanne to dinner, much as she wanted to meet him, it would mean that she would not be able to keep her promise to Pierre Valéry.

However, there was nothing she could say, and after an excellent luncheon cooked by Marie the Duke said:

"I am now going to the Inn. You had better wait here until I return, and while you are waiting you can finish your painting of the view from the garden."

"Yes, of course, Papa," Simonetta agreed.

The Duke went striding away towards the Inn, a smile on his lips which told Simonetta that he was looking forward to meeting Cézanne, whose paintings he had described to her so often.

She waited until he was out of sight, then hurried after him in the same direction because to reach the Inn he had to pass the Temple of Love.

She hoped and almost prayed that Pierre Valéry would be there, but she was a little afraid that he too might have gone away for a meal and she would miss him.

But her prayers were unnecessary and once again when she could see round the trees he was sitting in the same place at his easel, and as she ran towards him and he rose to his feet she knew that he was glad to see her.

"I had to ... come and tell you what is ... happening," she said a little breathlessly as she reached him.

"I have been hoping that you would do so," he said simply. "But what has happened?"

"My master has gone to the Inn to ask Paul Cézanne, who is expected here today, to dine with us tonight."

"And you think that will prevent you from coming to model for me?" Pierre Valéry asked.

"I am ... afraid so."

"There seem to be a great many obstacles to prevent me from finishing my painting."

"I am sorry ... so very sorry."

"It is not your fault," he said, "but I cannot help being disappointed."

"Yes, of course," she agreed, "and I hope we can manage something, but at the moment I am not certain when it will be."

"In the meantime," he said, "how did you enjoy yourself last night with the *Comte?*"

He saw the answer on her face before she turned her head away and said:

"It was horrible!"

Pierre Valéry was still. Then he asked sharply:

"What happened?"

Too late Simonetta realised it would have been better not to confide in anybody, least of all a stranger.

"It is . . . not important," she said. "Let me look at your painting."

"Tell me what happened. I want to know!"

Simonetta shook her head.

"No, it is . . . best not to . . . speak about it."

"I insist!" Pierre Valéry said. "Look at me, Simonetta!"

She did not move, her eyes fixed on the Temple of Love, the sunshine making the pale stones glow with the translucence of a pearl.

"I think," he said quietly after a moment's silence, "that something occurred which shocked you."

She was surprised that he was so perceptive. At the same time, she thought it would be humiliating to tell him what the *Comte* had suggested.

"I do not . . . want to . . . talk about it."

"I warned you to beware of wolves in sheep's clothing!"

"I knew you were . . . right after it had . . . happened," she murmured.

"What happened?"

This time his question seemed to ring out like a challenge.

Then as she did not reply he put his hands on her shoulders and turned her round to face him.

"Look at me," he said, "and tell me, because it is important for me to know, what has upset and shocked you."

"I do not . . . want you to know."

"Did he touch you?" Pierre Valéry asked. "If he did —I swear I will kill him!"

The way he spoke was so surprising that Simonetta looked up into his eyes, then was unable to look away.

"Did he?"

"No . . . no," she answered. "It was just that he . . . suggested something . . . wrong and wicked . . . and I did not know that . . . men were like that."

She could see that Pierre Valéry looked somewhat bewildered before he asked:

"Like what?"

"The *Comte* . . . suggested taking . . . me to Paris . . . and buying me . . . jewels . . . !"

Her voice seemed to trail away a little incoherently, Then she added:

"He had only . . . seen me once . . . before!"

"What did you answer him?" Pierre Valéry enquired.

His hands were still on her shoulders and she could feel the strength of his fingers through her gown.

Simonetta had the idea that because he was so strong he could protect her against the *Comte* or anything else that frightened or threatened her.

He waited for her to reply and after a moment she said:

"I did not have to . . . say anything . . . my . . . Master came back into the Salon with the *Comte's* sister, who was also . . . there."

Although he did not say anything, it was obvious that Pierre Valéry was angry. After a moment he said:

"You must not see him again!"

"I hope I never do!" Simonetta said fervently. "And as my Master does not wish to see him either, I shall try to forget that he . . . insulted me."

There was silence. Then Pierre Valéry said:

"I cannot understand why your parents, if you have any, allow you first of all to become an Art Student, without seeing that you are properly looked after, or why you are allowed to come away to France with an elderly man, which is bound to give people the wrong idea about you."

"The wrong idea?" Simonetta repeated. "What do you mean by that? What wrong ideas can they have when I am with my Master?"

There was a little pause before Pierre Valéry said, as if he was choosing his words carefully:.

"I am referring to the ideas which occurred to the *Comte* because he thought your life was rather different from what it actually is."

As if she was tired of standing, Simonetta sat down on the grass beside Pierre Valéry's easel.

"I do not . . . understand what you are . . . saying."

Pierre Valéry smiled, then he sat down on his stool.

"Let us talk about something else," he said. "I am quite certain you find the *Comte* as boring a subject as I do."

"I never want to think about him again!" Simonetta said passionately.

"Then let us talk about something really interesting," he said, "like the Temple I am trying to paint with you standing in the doorway."

Simonetta looked at it and smiled.

"It is so beautiful," she said. "I was just saying to my Master at luncheon that while I am here I want to learn more about the Troubadours and their songs and poems."

"Unfortunately, there was very little written down at the time, so there is not much left for us to study."

"That is very . . . disappointing."

"What I find so interesting," Pierre Valéry said, "is that it was the Troubadours of Provence who really discovered love."

Simonetta looked at him in surprise and asked:

"What do you mean by that?"

"At the dawn of the Middle Ages," he answered, "love did not play a very important part in society, and it was in fact the Troubadours of Provence whose poems and songs introduced it to France."

"How fascinating!" Simonetta exclaimed. "I had no idea of that!"

France became the acknowledged leader of *ars amandi* and of love itself; a position from which she has never been ousted."

Simonetta clasped her hands together.

"This is what I wished to know! Please tell me more."

Even as she spoke she looked over her shoulder, afraid that she would see her father walking down the road, returning from the Inn.

She rose to her feet.

"I cannot stay now," she said, "but I will come back to hear more."

"If you do not do so, you will upset me considerably," Pierre Valéry said, "and you are also aware that without you my painting is ruined."

"Do not look at it like that," Simonetta pleaded. "I promise I will do my very, very best to come to you when I can."

She hesitated before she asked:

"If you go anywhere else . . . you will let me . . . know?"

"Of course."

"I will come as soon as it is possible."

She would have walked away, but he said quickly:

"Wait a minute!"

She paused and looked up at him.

"What I am going to suggest," he said, "is that you join me tonight, or perhaps tomorrow night, so that I can show you Les Baux by moonlight."

"How can I do that?" Simonetta asked, almost as if she relied on him to have the answer.

Pierre Valéry thought for a moment.

"Perhaps after dinner your Master will go back with Cézanne to the Inn to join the other artists. Alternatively, if he is asleep you might come to me."

"It will be difficult," Simonetta said, "but I do want to see the moonlight on the rocks."

"Then I shall wait here for you," he said, "until I am

quite certain it is too late and impossible for you to come."

"Thank you. You are very . . . very . . . kind."

She smiled at him.

Then she was running away, moving swiftly through the grass to jump lithely over the lavender hedge and disappear out of sight behind the trees.

Pierre Valéry watched her go without moving.

Then several minutes later with a little sigh he sat down at his easel and began to paint.

* * *

Looking at Paul Cézanne across the table, Simonetta thought that he had an extremely interesting face.

His high forehead, from which his hair receded, made him look very intelligent, and although his beard obscured a great deal of his face, his eyes, dark and mystic, gave her the feeling that he lived in a world of his own.

He had a strange voice because he articulated his words carefully in an Aixois accent, which contrasted with his exaggeratedly polite manners.

He was the sort of man that Simonetta knew her father would refer to as a "real person."

The things he said and the new ideas he expounded over dinner were, she thought, exactly what her father wished to hear from the painters who lived in a totally different world from the one he himself normally occupied.

Cézanne's ideas ranged over so many different themes that Simonetta listened with close attention, realising that this evening was something to remember when she returned to England and became a conventional débutante who was expected to think of nothing but enjoying herself.

She gathered from the artist that he despised society and even the company of his contemporary artists and was in many ways a "Lone Wolf."

As the evening progressed, Simonetta thought that Cézanne was indeed a strange man, unpredictable and wholly unusual, yet she could understand that her father valued his friendship and was therefore flattered when Cézanne said:

"I only came here to see you. Tomorrow I shall return to Aix. I found those blockheads and their pretentions over their paintings intolerable!"

When dinner was over Simonetta tried not to think of Pierre Valéry waiting for her. Then after a while Cézanne grew restless and said to the Duke:

"I suppose I had better return to the Inn and see if my so-called friends have found me somewhere to sleep."

"I wish I could offer you a bed," the Duke replied regretfully, "but alas, we have only two rooms."

"I shall be all right," Cézanne replied. "Come, Calvert, let us walk back in the moonlight and drink in the beauty of it before we have to listen to the postulating of those who think they know all about nature."

The Duke laughed and rose to his feet.

Cézanne bade Simonetta good-night and went ahead, while the Duke stayed back for a moment to say:

"Go to bed, my child. I will try not to wake you when I get back, which I expect will be late."

"Enjoy yourself, Papa."

Then her father hurried out after Paul Cézanne, who was already walking down the road.

Simonetta waited for a little while until they would be out of sight, then knew that this was the opportunity she wanted to join Pierre Valéry and see the moonlight.

She was sure that she would be back before her father returned.

At the same time, she flattered herself that she was being very practical when she took with her the key from the back-door, just in case he came in first and bolted the one they habitually used.

"Considering that I have never been left on my own

before," she said to herself, "I am really doing very well."

She almost wished she could boast of her cleverness, then knew she must not speak to anybody about the part she was playing.

"I am an Art Student," she told herself. "I am here on my own, and therefore it is not in the least reprehensible that I should go look at the moonlight with another painter."

Brave words, but at the same time her conscience pricked her uncomfortably because she knew she was deceiving her father in doing something of which he would most violently disapprove.

"He would not disapprove of Pierre Valéry as much as he would of the *Comte* if he knew of his behaviour," she argued to herself.

At the same time, afraid that her upbringing would prevail against her imagination, she ran down the road as if she was escaping not only from the house but from herself.

When she reached the lavender hedge, Pierre Valéry was beside her.

He had obviously been waiting in the shadows of the trees, and because he appeared unexpectedly Simonetta gave a little exclamation.

"I did not mean to frighten you," he said quickly, "but I saw the two men walking towards the Inn, and waited in case you were brave enough to join me as you promised to do."

"I am . . . here," Simonetta said in a small voice.

"Yes, and I am very grateful that you are. Come along! We have a lot to see and enjoy before you must return."

He put his hand under her elbow, and it seemed a very natural thing for him to do.

He drew her a little way down the road, then turned off up a small winding path which gradually climbed higher and higher until it became steps.

She realised they were ascending the side of the rocks on which the Castle had originally been built.

It was quite a hard climb, and in the shadows of the trees which bordered the path, Simonetta would have found it difficult to find her way if Pierre Valéry had not held her by the hand.

Higher and higher they climbed until suddenly they were in the moonlight and Les Baux lay beneath them, the rocks gleaming luminously with an indescribable beauty, deep and mysterious.

Above them the ruins of the Castle seemed to combine with the magic which radiated from it and through them like a magnet.

Afterwards Simonetta felt that she herself had been enchanted and that she had stepped back into the past.

She thought the Castle was inhabited by feudal Princes, fiery-souled, swift-handed, who claimed their descent from Balthazar, one of the Magi, bearing on their coat-of-arms the Star of the East.

They were attended by beautiful women wearing gowns with long sleeves, their hair bound with pearls, and serenaded by Troubadours whose boots ended in a curved peak.

They sang of love, and the wonder of it vibrated on the atmosphere, but Simonetta was not really certain if it was the Troubadours she heard or Pierre Valéry who recited their poems and songs to her, one of which began:

> *"I think of her so much and love her so truly*
> *That night and day I tremble at my thoughts."*

Pierre's voice was very low and deep and seemed part of the dark shadows and as unreal as the moon itself.

After a long silence when the only sound was the

faraway croaking of the bull-frogs in the ponds in the valley, he went on:

"And since Love so wished to honour me
As to let me bear you in my heart,
I beg of you to keep it from the flames,
Since I fear for you.
Much more than for myself."

They walked on what had been the ramparts and stood looking over the wind-tormented plain of Avignon and in the distance La Camargue with its salt-pools left by a lingering sea, gleaming like a silver thread.

Beyond where they were standing, Les Alpilles, silver-blue in the moonlight, stretched away in a rugged silhouette which seemed to blend with the sky.

Then gently Pierre took Simonetta by the arm and drew her back down the way they had come, his hand holding hers, so that in the darkness she felt as if he were taking her away from a Paradise and into a world she had no wish to remember.

Only when the house with its red roof was just ahead of them did she feel they could speak normally to each other, even though they had been talking for a long time without words.

"Now you have seen Les Baux by moonlight," Pierre Valéry said softly.

"I shall never . . . forget."

"Of course not," he replied. "I have given it to you as a present, and nothing and nobody can take it from your heart."

"How can you . . . understand that is what I feel?" she enquired.

"Because it is what I feel myself, and to be with you on such a night is something I will always remember."

"So will I," Simonetta said.

They were standing in the moonlight as she looked

up into his face, trying to find words in which to express her feelings.

Her eyes met his and she had the feeling that he wanted to kiss her.

She knew she had never known such ecstasy before and perhaps would never know it again.

They stood looking at each other, and Simonetta waited, finding it almost impossible to breathe.

Then sharply, in a voice that seemed to grate and break the fragility of the spell that had bound them indivisibly to each other, Pierre Valéry said:

"Now we must say good-night and you must go to bed, Simonetta."

It was almost as if he had thrown a glass of cold water in her face!

She felt as if she wanted to cry out to him for having destroyed something so precious, so indefinably rapturous, that it seemed almost a crime to have done so.

She put up her hands in protest as if he had struck her, but already he was walking away towards the house and there was nothing she could do but follow him.

"Please, Pierre . . . wait for me!" she cried, feeling as if he would disappear and she would never know again the rapture she had been feeling.

She realised that this was the first time she had used his Christian name, although he had used hers.

He waited, and she thought the expression in his eyes had changed.

There was a darkness in them, and he was frowning,
Suddenly she felt very young and lost.

"What has . . . happened? What have I . . . done? Why have you . . . altered?"

"You must go to bed," he said. "It is too late for you to be out."

Again he was moving away from her, and she asked herself despairingly what could have upset him, as she followed him through the open gate into the garden and up the little path that led to the front door.

Pierre stood at the door as if waiting to say good-night to her.

Then she saw that it was open, although she had left it shut, and she thought with a constriction of her heart that her father had returned.

It flashed through her mind that he would be very, very angry, and she drew in her breath as if it would give her courage.

Then as she did so, somebody inside the house rose from the chair in which he had been sitting and came walking towards her, and she saw who it was.

It was the *Comte!*

For a moment Simonetta felt that her eyes were deceiving her.

Then putting out his hand the *Comte* pulled the door open wider in front of her.

"I was waiting for you," he said. "Where have you been? And who is this?"

He stared in a hostile manner at Pierre Valéry, who answered:

"The real question is—why are you here and what right have you to be waiting for *Mademoiselle?*"

"I have no idea who you are," the *Comte* answered aggressively, "but as my business is with *Mademoiselle*, I suggest you leave! And the quicker the better!"

Simonetta gave a little cry.

"No . . . please . . . he is not to go . . . and I cannot entertain you, *Monsieur*, in my . . . Master's absence."

In her confusion once again she had almost said "father," but at the last minute had managed to prevent herself from saying anything so revealing.

The *Comte* moved back into the Sitting-Room, where there were several lighted candles.

"Come in, Simonetta!" he said in a voice of authority. "Then I can shut the door on this impertinent fellow who has brought you home."

Simonetta looked at Pierre Valéry appealingly and he

walked ahead of her into the Sitting-Room to stand facing the *Comte*.

He was the taller of the two, and Simonetta felt with relief that at least he would be able to protect her.

Slowly, because she was so nervous, she followed and stood back while the two men eyed each other like fighting cocks—neither of them speaking, but waiting, it seemed, for the first move.

The *Comte* spoke.

"I told you to leave."

"I have no intention of doing so until you have gone."

"That is for me to decide," the *Comte* answered, "and I am not taking orders from any riff-raff who has no right to associate with *Mademoiselle* in her teacher's absence."

"Do not let us bandy words," Pierre Valéry replied. "Are you leaving, *Monsieur le Comte*, or must I throw you out?"

There was a flash of fury on the *Comte's* face as he answered:

"You apparently know who I am, in which case you know I have influence not only here but also in Paris. Either you get out, or I promise you I will see to it that you never sell a painting again!"

"You are trying to blackmail me," Pierre Valéry said, "which does not surprise me. It only confirms my opinion that you are not the sort of man who should be left alone with a young woman!"

"You scum! You rat from the gutter! I will not put up with your insults!" the *Comte* roared.

As he spoke he made a menacing gesture towards Pierre Valéry, which was what he was waiting for.

He seized the *Comte's* raised arm and, holding him in a grip which rendered him completely helpless, propelled him across to the door and outside into the garden.

The *Comte* struggled to free himself, at the same time uttering a stream of oaths. He was in fact so astonished at being manhandled that when Pierre Valéry released him he stumbled and fell, and lay on the garden path outraged and furious.

Then as he gasped for breath, the door was slammed to and he heard an iron bolt shot into place.

Inside, Pierre Valéry stood with his back against the door looked at Simonetta, who, with her hands clasped together, was trembling at what had just occurred.

At the same time her eyes were shining.

All she could think of was that Pierre had saved her from the *Comte* and she did not have to be alone with him.

Then as the horror of what had happened swept over her, she gave a little cry that seemed almost stifled on her lips, and threw herself against Pierre.

She felt his arms go round her.

Then as she looked up at him, wanting to thank him for saving her, his lips came down on hers.

Chapter Five

For a moment all Simonetta could think of was that Pierre's arms were strong and protective and she was safe.

Then the pressure of his lips on hers made her feel as if he gave her the moonlight and the magic that they had been watching at the Castle.

He took her into the fairy-land that she had longed for and dreamt of and which was part of the Troubadours and the love he said they had brought to France.

It was so perfect and so wonderful that she felt as if she were no longer human but disembodied. She was not a ghost, but her whole being was pulsating with light and she was high above the world and one with the gods.

Pierre's arms tightened and he held her even closer, and he kissed her until Simonetta thought he had taken her heart and her soul from her and made them his.

It was so perfect, so glorious, and at the same time so sacred and divine that she knew this was what the Impressionists tried to portray in their paintings—this was the light of love, which came from God.

How long Pierre kissed her she had no idea.

She knew only that the rapture and ecstasy of it was

out of time and might have lasted a few seconds or many centuries.

What he was giving to and taking from her was love—love that was eternal and could never die.

Only when she felt it was impossible for anybody to feel such beauty and not faint with the wonder of it did Pierre raise his head.

"*Ma chérie!*" he said in a voice that she barely recognised. "I did not mean this to happen."

Simonetta made an inarticulate little sound of protest because he had taken his lips from hers, then as if she suddenly became herself and realised that she had been kissed, she hid her face against his shoulder.

He held her very close and she had the feeling that he was battling with himself, although why he should, she could not understand.

Then at last he said:

"This is wrong, and I should have gone away when we first met."

She did not understand, but she raised her face to say:

"I did not know . . . I never guessed a . . . kiss could be so wonderful . . . so perfect!"

"Is that what it was for you?" he asked.

"It was like the . . . moonlight . . . like the . . . light you try to paint . . . now I understand what it . . . means to you."

Her voice trembled with the intensity of her feelings, and after a moment he said:

"You have never been kissed before?"

"No . . . of course . . . not."

"Oh, my darling, that is what I thought."

Then he was kissing her again, his lips passionate, insistent, demanding, and she surrendered herself to him so completely that she felt as if her body melted into his . . . .

A long time later, Pierre raised his head to say:

"I must leave you. Your Master must not come back and find me here."

Simonetta gave a little cry.

"Supposing the . . . *Comte* returns!"

She felt as if she had come back from the stars to face the problems that had been there before Pierre had lifted her into the sky with his kisses.

Now once again she was afraid, and she clung to him, shivering as she said:

"Please . . . do not leave me . . . I am afraid of the . . . *Comte!*"

"He will not hurt you," Pierre said quietly. "That I promise you. I will watch from outside the house because I think there is too much explaining to do, and I know you are tired."

There was a consideration and an understanding in the way he spoke which made Simonetta feel as if he protected and looked after her.

She gave a little sigh and put her head down again on his shoulder.

"Supposing you had not . . . been here with . . . me?" she whispered.

"But I was," he replied. "Now I want you to go to sleep, my precious one. Tomorrow come to me when you can, and we will try to talk sensibly about what we can do."

"I want . . . you to . . . kiss me," Simonetta whispered.

"I want that too," Pierre answered, "but I also have to look after you. That is why I must protect you not only from the *Comte* but from myself."

She felt his lips against her hair as he said:

"Although it is an agony to go, I must leave you. Good-night, my precious little Venus, and do not worry about anything."

He took his arms from round her as he spoke, and she gave a little cry.

"Promise you will not . . . go away . . . just in case . . . "

"You are quite safe," he interrupted. "Do not think of

anything except the beauty we have seen tonight and the wonder of your first kiss."

As he stood looking at her in the light of the candles, he said almost as if he spoke to himself:

"How can you be so beautiful and at the same time pure and untouched?"

Simonetta stood irresolute for a moment.

Then because she knew without further words what he wanted of her, she gave him a faint smile and turned and went up the narrow staircase to her bedroom.

When she reached it she knew that Pierre had not moved but was waiting downstairs until she was safely in her room.

She wanted to run down to him again, to hold on to him and ask him to kiss her just once more.

Then, with what was a superhuman effort, she went into her bedroom and shut the door behind her.

She stood listening and after a moment she heard Pierre walk towards the front door, open it, go out, and pull it to behind him.

Her bedroom window looked out in the opposite direction, so that she could see him in the garden.

But she knew without seeing him that he would do as he said and watch the house until her father returned, and she need not be afraid.

Slowly, almost as if she were in a dream, Simonetta undressed.

It was only when she was in bed that she felt that everything that had happened must have been part of a dream.

It was too perfect and too wonderful to be reality.

Then she heard the front door open and close and knew that her father had returned.

* * *

Simonetta awoke with a feeling that she had been dreaming of something so wonderful that she wanted to hold on to it with both hands and not let it escape her.

Then she remembered what had happened the night before and felt the rapture of Pierre's kiss seep over her so that she imagined that she was still in his arms and his lips were on hers.

"I love him!" she told herself.

She wondered if he was thinking of her and feeling the same.

Then as she thought back over what had happened, she found that some of the things he had said puzzled her.

At the same time, it was difficult to recall anything but the rapture he had given her and the feeling that she had found the light which had inspired the Impressionists and had been part of the moonlight she had seen on the rocks.

"How could anything be more wonderful or beautiful?" she asked herself.

She knew that the only thing that mattered was that Pierre should give her the same feeling again and that she should make sure that he loved her.

She dressed quickly, feeling that the sunshine was brighter than it had ever been before, and the scent of the flowers was almost overwhelming.

She felt as if she pulsated with a new life that made her want to dance and sing and float up into the sky.

She went out of the house and into the garden. The rocks seemed to be glowing with a new luminosity, and she wished she could capture their magic and portray it on canvass with a genius that would make their beauty live forever.

She was thinking of the light when her father joined her.

"You are up very early, my dearest," he said, "but it will give us more time for painting."

With an effort Simonetta came back from the fairyland in which she had been day-dreaming to ask:

"Did you enjoy yourself last night, Papa?"

"It was very interesting," the Duke replied. "Cézanne

talked, and it was almost a lecture to some of the young artists who are here for the first time. I found what he had to say most educational and enlightening."

"It sounds very interesting, Papa."

"I will tell you about it later," the Duke said. "Now I want my breakfast. I only hope Marie will not keep us waiting."

Marie was already coming from the kitchen, smiling as she put a small basket of hot *croissants* on the table.

There was also a large pat of golden yellow butter, a pot of steaming coffee, and some of the special honey of Provence which Simonetta thought had a taste and a fragrance all its own.

They ate the *croissants* in silence until the Duke said:

"I have finished my painting, and I have found another place a little distance away where there is a view of the rocks that interests me."

As he spoke, Simonetta realised that if they went farther from the house she would also be farther from Pierre.

"I have not finished my painting yet, Papa."

"You are taking a long time over it," the Duke said. "Show me what you have done so far."

A little reluctantly, because she was afraid that perhaps he would think she had wasted her time, Simonetta fetched her canvass.

He looked at it and smiled.

"I see you are trying to copy Monet," he said. "It is not a bad effort, but I suggest that while he is an artist I greatly admire, it would be more in character if you followed your own instinct, your own perception, and paint it as you want to rather than as you think you should."

Simonetta laughed.

"You are so clever, Papa. I am sure you are right, and that is what I will try to do. I have spoilt that painting anyway."

She took it from him, put it down in a corner, and picked up one of the new canvasses they had brought with them.

"The great thing about painting," she said, "is that one can always go back to the beginning."

"Which unfortunately is something we cannot do in our ordinary lives," the Duke said drily.

Simonetta thought she had no wish to forget what had happened last night, nor to begin again her friendship, if that was the right word, with Pierre.

It was so wonderful, so perfect as it was, that she would not have missed one moment of it.

But where the *Comte* was concerned, she wished that somehow she could erase him from her mind with a stroke of her brush and be sure that she had in fact never met him.

Even to think of him made her shiver, and she hoped that after what had happened last night he would no longer wish to know her and would cease to pursue her.

That would be the best thing that could happen, but she had the uncomfortable feeling that because he had been made to look a fool by Pierre, he would seek his revenge.

"Supposing he hurts him?" Simonetta worried to herself. "He really meant it when he said he would see that Pierre never sells a painting again."

She wondered how she could prevent that from happening, then suddenly she felt afraid.

She had been so happy with her feelings on waking, remembering only the magical kisses she had received from Pierre.

Now like a dark cloud obscuring the light from the sun there was the *Comte*.

"What shall I do?" Simonetta asked herself, and wondered if after all it would be wisest to tell her father what had happened.

Then she knew that he would not only be horrified

but would tell her to pack her box immediately and perhaps not even allow her to say good-bye to Pierre.

'I dare not tell him,' she thought.

The Duke was collecting his easel and his paints.

"Come on," he said. "We have quite a walk to the place where I want to start my new painting, and when I mentioned it to Cézanne he said it was a scene he had always wanted to paint himself."

Simonetta knew that in that case nothing she could say would change her father's mind, so she picked up her paints and her new canvass to follow him through the garden.

They walked to a place where the rocks rose sharply on one side and on the other was a small stream meandering between bushes that were in blossom, making a picture that could not fail to be the delight of any artist.

It took the Duke a little time to arrange his easel in exactly the position he wished, and when he was settled, Simonetta, knowing he did not like to feel encroached on, walked some yards away from him and set up her own easel.

Only when she began to paint was she aware that it was difficult to think of anything but Pierre, the strength of his arms and the touch of his lips.

He had given her an ecstasy which she was sure was more wonderful than anything anyone had ever known before in this world.

"I must see him," she told herself. "I must see him so that we can talk as he said he wanted to."

Once again fate stepped in to help her.

When they returned to the house for luncheon, Marie as she brought in the delicious dishes she had cooked for them said:

"It is going to be very hot this afternoon. I have never known the sun to be so strong at this time of the year. *M'mselle* would be wise after luncheon to rest until it grows cooler."

"That is not a bad idea," the Duke said. "Why do you not lie down for a little while before you join me?"

Simonetta's heart leapt.

"Are you quite sure you will not be lonely without me, Papa?"

Her father smiled.

"Even though I am not particularly communicative while I am painting," he said, "I still like to have you with me and to know you are there. At the same time, I do not wish you to over-tire yourself."

As he spoke he looked at her, then he added:

"You certainly look very well, but painting can take a lot out of one, and you have been working hard ever since we came here."

"Then I will do as you suggest," Simonetta said, "and wait until it grows cooler."

"That is a sensible child," the Duke approved.

He did not linger over his coffee but set off eagerly to get back to his painting.

Simonetta went up the stairs and lay down on her bed until she heard Marie finish washing and cleaning in the kitchen and shut the back-door behind her.

Then Simonetta jumped up, and after giving Marie time to walk back along the road which led to the village, she ran as quickly as she could towards the Temple of Love.

Pierre was there as she knew he would be.

As she hurried towards him through the flower-filled grass she felt her heart beating in her breast and knew that she had never been so excited and thrilled in her whole life as she was now because she was seeing him again.

She put out her hands towards him.

"Oh . . . Pierre . . . !"

He stood looking at her, then he took her hands and kissed them one after the other.

"Last night was true . . . it was true . . . was it not?" Simonetta asked.

"Very true for me," Pierre replied, "but I have to talk to you."

"It is what you said you wanted to do. I was able to come because my Master thought that as it was so hot I should lie down."

"Whatever the reason, I am grateful you are here."

"It is more wonderful than I can possibly tell you to know that I am with you . . . and you make me feel . . . safe."

Pierre's hands tightened on hers. Then he said:

"Sit down, *ma chérie*, I have to talk to you and it is not going to be easy."

There was a note in his voice which made Simonetta look at him a little sharply.

"It is not . . . the *Comte?* He is not making . . . trouble for you?"

"No, no! Forget him!" Pierre replied. "He cannot hurt me."

"He may do . . . and that is what frightens me," Simonetta said. "He may prevent you from selling your paintings, and that would be disastrous!"

"I told you, he is not important, except when he frightens you."

Simonetta drew in her breath.

"He does . . . frighten me," she said, "but I am able to go back to England . . . while you will be in Paris."

She looked up at him with worried eyes, and Pierre said:

"You are thinking of me! Can anybody be so wonderful?"

"Of course I am thinking of you," Simonetta said. "You threw him out of the house to save me, and I know it is something he will never forgive. He is vengeful and wicked! I think I was aware of it the first moment I met him."

Pierre sighed.

"I am afraid you will find that a great many men are what you call 'wicked' where you are concerned."

"Why?" Simonetta asked.

Pierre smiled.

"Because, my darling, you are so beautiful, and when men desire beauty they lose their heads and often behave like animals."

"That is what the *Comte* was . . . doing last night," Simonetta said in a low voice, "but as I said, I can escape, while . . . you cannot."

"Forget about me," Pierre said, "even though I am deeply grateful for your concern. What we have to discuss, Simonetta, is what we can do about—us."

"What can we do?" Simonetta asked.

There was silence. Then Pierre said in a voice that somehow seemed strange:

"I tried not to love you. I knew when I first saw you standing in the Temple of Love that you glowed with a light which held and enchanted me and it would be impossible for me to escape."

"Did I really do . . . that?"

"I promise you that is the truth."

"And when you came towards me," Simonetta said slowly, "I felt that you were different from any man I had ever talked to before, and I could trust you."

Pierre made a sound that was almost like a groan.

"That is what you should have been able to do, but I have failed you."

Simonetta looked at him startled.

"But . . . how? she asked. "You saved me from the *Comte* . . . you protected me and . . ."

Suddenly she felt shy and looked down.

There was a little silence. Then she said:

"I . . . I do not think I can . . . say it . . ."

Pierre sat down on the grass beside her and reached out to take her hand, then holding it tightly in his he said:

"Tell me what you were going to say."

Because he was touching her and she could feel the

vibrations she had felt before coming from his fingers, Simonetta looked up and felt herself quiver.

At the same time, the rapture he had given her last night was rising again in her breast, moving almost like a shaft of sunlight up her throat and into her lips.

She raised her eyes and felt no longer shy but spellbound.

"Y-you gave me...love!" she whispered.

"Oh, my darling," Pierre said in his deep voice. "If I gave you love, you gave me the perfection of the Divine, the light I have always sought and thought never to find."

As he was speaking he raised her hand to his lips and kissed it.

Simonetta's fingers clung to his as if she felt she could never let him go. Then she said:

"I know what we feel for each other is the love the Troubadours sang about in their songs, a love both ... spiritual and ... perfect."

"That is what you are," Pierre said, "and that is why I must go away."

Simonetta looked at him as if she could not understand what he had said. Then she said with a little cry:

"Why must you go away? You cannot leave me! Please ... please ... you cannot leave me—! Supposing the *Comte* ..."

"I will make sure the *Comte* does not trouble you again," Pierre said. "At the same time, as I cannot allow myself to hurt or to spoil you, my precious little Venus, I have to leave you."

"I ... I do not ... understand."

He looked at her eyes, which were perplexed and a little frightened as a child's might be, and said:

"You are not only all the temptations of St. Anthony, my precious, but you are also an idealist, as I am, and I cannot let myself spoil you."

"But . . . why should you spoil me? Are you . . . saying that . . . our love is . . . wrong?"

Before he could answer, Simonetta asked quickly:

"You are not . . . married, like the *Comte?*"

Pierre shook his head.

"No, I am not married."

Simonetta was silent. It suddenly struck her that what she wanted more than anything else in the world was to be married to Pierre, to be his wife.

Now she understood it; it came to her almost like a revelation what real love was, and that what she had found in Pierre was the love that her father wished her to have for the man who would be her husband.

Then as the truth swept over her, she knew that because she was who she was, never in any circumstances would she be allowed to marry an impecunious artist.

Because the emotions she felt had swept her into a fantasy-land, because even this morning when she awoke she had really not understood the full implication of her happiness or the love the Pierre had awakened in her, she had not until this moment connected it with marriage or even with her own future.

Now she knew that she would never find happiness, never be complete, unless she could be with Pierre.

But she also knew that such an idea was so alien to all her upbringing, to everything that had been in her life until she had come to Les Baux, that for a moment she could not adjust herself to the strangeness of it.

If she was silent, Pierre was silent too.

He was staring across at the Temple of Love as if he felt it could solve his problem for him, and yet had little hope that it could do so.

Holding on to Pierre's hand as if it were a lifeline in a rough sea, Simonetta said as the silence between them became oppressive:

"Must we . . . try to make a . . . decision now? I was so

happy last night ... when there were no ... problems and no ... difficulties."

"There is the problem of you," Pierre replied. "I told myself I would not tell you what I felt about you, and most important of all I would not touch you. But what happened knocked me off my balance, and I am ashamed at my lack of self-control."

Simonetta turned to him wide-eyed. Then she said in a very small voice:

"You are ... you are not ... sorry you ... kissed me?"

There was a flicker of pain in her eyes, as if the mere idea hurt her intolerably, and Pierre said quickly:

"No, of course not! If it was wonderful for you, my darling one, it was even more wonderful for me."

"It was so perfect ... so rapturous ... I felt as if we flew into the sky and were no longer human beings but perhaps ... one with the gods of Les Baux in Roman times."

"That is what I felt too," Pierre said.

"You are sure ... you are really sure ... and you are not saying so just to please me?"

"It would be impossible to describe to you what I felt," he replied, "and it is also something I must not do."

"Why not? I would like you to tell me."

"Because it means that we are slipping deeper and deeper into a kind of quicksand which is dangerous and from which I must save you, even from myself."

As he spoke to her there was a note in his voice that made Simonetta vibrate to it as if at the sound of music, the music which was part of the beat of her heart and the glory of the sun.

"How can you not ... wish to say it?" she whispered.

Pierre looked at her and gave a little groan.

"Oh, my precious Venus, you are so sweet, so unsophisticated and unspoilt. How is it possible for me to have met someone who could only have stepped out of a dream, but to know there is nothing I can do about it?"

It struck Simonetta that she could do nothing about it either, and yet it was something she could not say.

How could she go to her father and say that Pierre loved her and she loved him, knowing that at her first words her father would revert to being an autocratic Duke and no longer an Impressionist artist?

She would also have to admit that she had deceived not only her father but also Pierre. She could imagine how angry they both would be, and she would have little defence.

She thought wildly what she could do, but she was completely bewildered and found that because everything had happened so quickly, it was impossible to think clearly.

She could only clutch at her happiness.

"Please . . . please, Pierre," she begged, "can we not just for today be happy and try not to make . . . plans? I want to be with you. Please . . . say you want to be with me."

"You know I want that," Pierre replied roughly, "but I am trying to think of you."

"I am thinking of me too," Simonetta said, "and I want to see you . . . I must see you . . . please . . . for a little while . . . longer."

"Will that make it any easier when we have to say good-bye?"

The words: "Why must we say good-bye?" trembled on Simonetta's lips, but she dared not say them.

'Of course we have to say good-bye,' she thought to herself, 'and it will be better if I do not tell him who I am, but just go back with Papa to England and try to forget him.'

Then she knew that she would never forget Pierre.

She loved him, and although she was quite certain that people would say she was young and would get over what was her first love, she knew that was something which would never happen.

She was as sure as if somebody were telling her that the love she had for Pierre was a love that came only once in a lifetime. Whether he was aware of it or not, she would be his until she died.

Then she felt that it was all too big, too frightening for her to contemplate.

All she could be sure of was that Pierre was here for the moment. She could touch him, and tomorrow might never come.

"Please . . . Pierre . . . please," she pleaded, "let us be . . . happy."

He turned his face from the contemplation of the Temple to look at her.

"You know I am thinking of you."

"Then . . . please . . . do as I ask . . . I love you!"

As if the words she spoke so softly that he could barely hear them broke his resolve, he put his arms round her and pushed her backwards onto the grass.

Then he was kissing her—kissing her demandingly with a passion that was fiery and different from the way he had kissed her the night before.

Now he was a man, not a god, and she was a woman whom he desired and claimed as his own.

To Simonetta the magic and the rapture were there, and even though she knew that what he was feeling for her was different, it was still wonderful.

The fire on his lips awoke a tiny flicker of flame within herself which again was different from anything she had ever before experienced or imagined.

It was an ecstasy and yet at the same time it was exciting and strange.

Pierre kissed her until they both were breathless.

Then he raised his head to look down at her, her eyes shining, her lips parted, her breath coming quickly in little gasps.

He knew that because he had aroused her she had a new beauty.

He would have kissed her again, but because she was a little shy of the fire in his eyes and the feelings he had awakened in her, she put up her hands in protest as if to hold him away from her.

She was instantly free, and he said as if he spoke to himself:

"I must not frighten you."

"You did not . . . frighten me," Simonetta said, and her voice seemed to come from very far away. "But when you kiss me . . . like that, you make me feel very . . . strange."

"Strange?" he questioned.

"I cannot explain . . . it is wonderful . . . but I feel as if there are little flashes of lightning running through me."

Pierre smiled, and yet it was also a sigh.

"You are very young," he said, "and I must not forget it."

"Do you mean that if I were older I should not . . . feel like that?"

His smile deepened.

"You will feel like that and a great deal more as well, but that is something which I should not explain to you any more than I should make you feel as you do now."

Simonetta looked up at him.

"Why not? It is very wonderful . . . and I am sure it is part of the love that belongs to the . . . Temple."

Her eyes searched his face before she asked:

"That is true? It is not . . . wrong for me to . . . feel as I do?"

"No, my darling, it is not wrong," Pierre replied.

He had been half-lying on the grass beside her, but now he sat up.

"Where are you supposed to be this afternoon?" he asked.

It was quite an effort for Simonetta to remember, and she thought for a moment before she said:

"I told you, I was supposed to lie down and rest, then join my Master later. But there is no hurry."

"Do you want me to kiss you again?" Pierre asked.

He saw a sudden radiance on Simonetta's face that was dazzling.

"You know I do!"

"Oh, my sweet, you make it very hard for me," he replied.

Then he was kissing her again, but this time more gently, as if she were a flower that he was touching, at the same time afraid he might damage the fragile petals.

Then he lay down beside her, holding her in his arms, and laid his cheek against hers.

"Look at the light on the rocks," he said, "and remember that that is what we are seeking and what in our own way we have given each other."

His words moved her and Simonetta said:

"How could anybody really capture it on canvass or in any other way? We only know it is there . . . that we seek it . . . and we take it inside . . . ourselves."

She knew by the way that Pierre's arms tightened round her that he understood what she was trying to say, and she thought it would be impossible to find another man who thought as he did and could teach her as Pierre could do.

When she lost him it would not only be like losing part of herself but like going into a darkness which the sunlight could not penetrate.

"You are thinking unhappy thoughts," he said unexpectedly.

"How . . . do you know that?"

"I think I know everything about you," he said, "your thoughts, your feelings, and the little vibrations that emanate from you towards me which I can feel as if they were waves of light."

He felt Simonetta start and asked:

"Why did you do that?"

"Because when I first touched your hand I felt vibrations coming from your fingers," she said, "and I think I knew then that you were something . . . very special, and nobody else could . . . ever be the . . . same."

As she spoke she wanted to add: "And why should there be anybody else?"

She wanted to tell him how much she wanted to stay with him and be with him.

Then she realised that while she had been miserably aware that she could never marry him, he had not actually said that he wanted to marry her.

As she puzzled over it, she knew the reason.

It was because being a painter, he was too poor to keep a wife, and because he loved her he would not offer her a life of penury or the frustrations of his not being appreciated as an artist.

Her father had told her of how the Impressionists suffered, and she could understand that Pierre would be too noble to ask her to share such a life.

Then it struck her that if he believed her to be an Art Student, why should he think the life she was leading at the moment to be different from the life that he could offer her?

It all flashed through Simonetta's mind, and yet it was impossible for her to ask questions, knowing that she was hiding something about herself and that if she had secrets, so did Pierre.

But to be in his arms was the most wonderful thing she could imagine, with the blue sky above them, the soft grass beneath them, and from where they were lying they could see nothing but the tops of the bare rocks gleaming white in the sunlight.

Simonetta felt that this was a world of their own; a world of freedom where nothing human or horrible could encroach, and there was only Pierre and her love for him.

"Now you are thinking of me," he said softly.

"How can I think of anything else when I am so happy?" Simonetta asked. "At the same time, it is . . . frightening that you can read my thoughts."

"It is not so much your thoughts as your feelings," he said. "I can feel them vibrating towards mine, and when they link together, then we are one person. Oh, my precious, how can I let you go?"

It was a cry of agony and she turned sideways so that she could be a little closer to him, and with her arms round him she said:

"I love you . . . I love you . . . and whatever happens, I shall always know that you have given me something so precious . . . so sacred, that I shall always thank God on my knees for . . . having met you."

He did not move or reply, and because he was silent Simonetta raised her head a little to look at him.

His face was turned up towards the sky and his eyes were closed.

Even so, she could see an expression of pain which made him look different from the way he had looked before.

She did not understand why he should look like that or what was upsetting him.

In that moment she knew only that because she loved him she would give her life to prevent him from suffering.

Chapter Six

As Pierre did not speak and seemed to not pay any attention to what she had been saying, Simonetta suddenly felt frightened.

"Pierre!" she called insistently. "Pierre!"

He opened his eyes and lay for a moment looking at her.

Then he sat up and put out his arms to draw her closer so that she was sitting beside him.

Then, staring across the grass to the Temple of Love, Pierre said in a low voice:

"Listen to me, my darling. I am going to say good-bye, and then I shall leave Les Baux."

Simonetta gave a cry of protest.

"Leave . . . why? Is it . . . something I have . . . . done?"

"No, of course not," Pierre replied, "but we cannot go on like this."

"I cannot . . . bear you to . . . go."

"It is something I have to do, and one day you will understand."

"I want to understand now . . . how can we lose this . . . precious time . . . together?"

Her voice quivered on the word "precious" and she felt Pierre's arms tighten round her.

112

Then he said, still in the serious voice he had used before:

"There are moments in one's life which are perfect, beautiful, and, as you have said, precious."

His voice deepened as he went on:

"One moment which I shall never forget was when I first saw you standing in the doorway of the Temple and thought you could not be human but were an apparition from the past."

Simonetta thought that she, for her part, would never forget seeing him come towards her and the vibrations she had felt when he touched her hand. But she did not speak, and Pierre went on:

"Another was when we sat in the moonlight beneath the Castle and I thought we both had stepped back in time."

"That is ... what I thought ... too," Simonetta murmured. "I imagined I could .. see the Castle as it was in the past ... and hear the Troubadours ... singing their songs of love."

"Then later," Pierre continued as if she had not spoken, "although I tried not to touch you, I kissed you and knew that no man could be more fortunate, for I had found Heaven upon earth."

Simonetta laid her cheek against his.

"It was ... so perfect," she whispered. "How could I ever let ... another man kiss me, since from that moment I ... belonged to ... you?"

She felt Pierre stiffen as he said:

"You must not say such things."

"Why not ... when they are ... true?"

"Because you cannot give your heart to me, and I shall try to pray that you will find some other happiness."

"How can I do that when I can only be ... happy with ... you?"

"That is a question I cannot answer," Pierre replied. "It is also the reason why I must go away."

Simonetta wanted to protest. Then she knew there was really nothing she could say.

If Pierre had to go away, so indeed had she.

Then she wondered if she could suggest that she should go with him.

She need never tell him who she was, but could let him think for the rest of their lives that she was an Art Student who was of no consequence to anybody.

However, she was intelligent enought to realise that this idea was just a dream. In the sensation there would be if Lady Simonetta Terrington-Trench disappeared, the Police, alerted by her father, would soon find her.

Although she was a little vague about it, she thought that in such circumstances Pierre might be accused of an offence against the law in abducting her.

'I cannot . . . hurt him,' she thought to herself. 'I love him, and anyway he may suffer because of me if the *Comte* carries out his threat and prevents him from selling his paintings.'

She suddenly realised how reprehensible it was of her to continue to plead with Pierre to stay with her when he had told her he must leave.

She did not quite understand why he could not go on seeing her at least until she and her father left, but she knew he was thinking of her and not of himself, and he was wiser than she was.

As if he was aware that her attitude had changed, Pierre said:

"This has been a wonderful dream; a moment when we sailed on wings of ecstasy into a world of magic, and where we have found the love which all men and women seek but which so often eludes them."

There was a note of sadness in his voice which made Simonetta want to cry.

"When we grow old," Pierre went on, "we will look back on this perfect moment in our lives; we will think of the light on the rocks, and we will know we have been blessed because we have been permitted not only to see it but to feel it and to hold it forever in our hearts."

"I . . . love . . . you!"

"And I love you, my precious little Venus."

He looked at her and Simonetta thought that he would kiss her. But instead he drew her to her feet, and with his arms round her they walked slowly, very slowly, through the grass towards the road.

Only when they were within a few feet of the lane ahead did Pierre stop in the shadows of the trees and say softly:

"Look at me, Simonetta!"

She turned towards him and lifted her face, her eyes wide and apprehensive, her lips trembling a little.

He looked at her for a long moment. Then he said:

"You are so beautiful! So ridiculously, absurdly beautiful! I cannot bear to think what the future will hold for you."

Simonetta could not reply but could only stand there, feeling that his words made her tremble. At the same time, because of the depth of emotion in his voice, her heart was beating more quickly, almost as if he were kissing her.

"Promise me," Pierre said, "wherever you go, whatever you do, you will remember the love we have found. Never debase the memory of it or accept a second-best."

He waited, and because she knew that he wanted her to reply, she managed to stammer:

"I . . . I promise."

It was then, with his eyes still on her face, that he very slowly put his arms round her and drew her close to him.

He did not kiss her mouth as she expected, but moved his lips very slowly over her forehead, her eyes, the softness of her cheeks, and her small, pointed chin.

Then at last he kissed her, a kiss that seemed to her different in every way from those he had given her before.

It was almost as if they were no longer a man and a woman, and as if he kissed her not with his body but with his spirit and his soul.

Then she was free and he said hoarsely:

"Go quickly, my darling, while I can let you. And may God go with you, now and for all eternity."

As he spoke he turned away and started to walk back towards his easel, and Simonetta, feeling that there was something final and sacred in his farewell, could only obey him.

She felt numb with the emotions she had experienced and the way Pierre had forced his will upon her.

She climbed over the little lavender hedge, thinking it was for the last time.

Then she walked back towards the house, and although the sunshine was hot and brilliant, she felt that she was cold and was groping her way through a thick fog.

A darkness seemed to be creeping up from her heart into her mind until it enveloped her completely and there was no longer any light.

* * *

Afterwards, Simonetta could never remember exactly what happened.

She could vaguely recall lying on her bed, suffering an agony that was physical as well as mental, and feeling as if some part of her was dying slowly but irrevocably.

Then, telling herself that life must go on, she thought she would change her gown and join her father.

She looked for a long time at her reflection in the mirror in her bedroom.

She felt as if she had grown immeasurably older, and that when Pierre had left her he had taken her beauty with him, and now her face must look different with the life gone out of it.

However, she seemed to look very much as she had before, but all she could hear was Pierre's voice saying:

"You are so incredibly, unbelievably beautiful!"

She thought to herself that it was strange she did not cry. Perhaps that would come later, although for the moment her eyes were dry.

Yet, instead of a heart there was a lump in her breast which seemed to prevent her from feeling anything but pain and more pain.

Finally she made herself rise from the dressing-table, pick up her hat, and go down the stairs to collect her canvass, which had very little on it, her paint-box, and her palette.

She was just about to carry them outside, although it was now a wearisome effort when before it had been a joy, when to her surprise she saw her father coming in through the garden gate.

She waited until he was close to her before she asked:

"What has . . . happened, Papa? Why are you . . . back so . . . early?"

"It is in fact quite late," her father replied, "and I was already returning to the house when I met the postman on the road with a telegram for me."

"A telegram, Papa?"

"It is annoying, extremely annoying, but I am afraid we have to return to England tomorrow morning."

"But . . . why, Papa?"

"The telegram is from the House of Lords," the Duke explained, passing by her and going into the house to put down his canvass and paints.

"What has . . . happened?"

It was difficult for Simonetta to ask the question or to force herself to realise what her father was saying.

"It is infuriating that it should occur at this moment," he replied crossly, "but before I left I promised the

Prime Minister tht I would introduce his new Bill on
Education in the Lords if it was passed by the House of
Commons."

Simonetta did not speak, and the Duke put his easel
and stool down on the ground with a clatter.

"I was quite certain," he continued," that the Bill
would not pass the Commons at the First Reading, but
now it has done so, so I must go back. There is nothing
else I can do."

"No . . . of course not . . . Papa."

Simonetta felt as if her voice came from a long
distance away, and all she could think of was that if
Pierre was leaving, so was she and she must tell him so.

Then as her father went on talking in an irritated
voice, she thought there was nothing more that she and
Pierre could say to each other.

He would in fact be even more upset than he was
already if once again he had to go through the misery of
parting from her.

'He will never know what has happened to me,' she
thought.

But she knew that the same applied to her, and
although she would search every Art Gallery and seek
for mention of his name or his paintings in every
newspaper and magazine, they were as lost to each
other as if they both had died.

Because her father told her to do so, she went
upstairs and started to pack her trunk, and she knew by
the sounds beneath her that he was doing the same.

She had not finished, in fact there were still several
gowns hanging in the wardrobe, when her father called
up the stairs that dinner was ready.

Simonetta had been so engrossed in her thoughts and
her misery that she had not realised that the sun had
sunk below the horizon, although there was still a
brilliant light on the top of the rocks.

Only to look at them was to feel a pain like that of a
dagger striking her.

She turned away to hurry down the stairs, determined not to look again at the light which brought Pierre so vividly into her mind that she felt she must cry out his name aloud.

Marie had cooked one of her delicious dinners, but as far as Simonetta was concerned she might have been eating sawdust.

As she listened to her father talking, she thought it was somebody else who made dutiful responses while she herself was no longer in her body but was far away, searching for Pierre to ask him on her knees not to leave her.

Then as dinner came to an end her father said:

"We have had a good holiday together, Simonetta, and I have enjoyed having you with me."

"Thank you . . . Papa."

"We must steal another one sometime," he went on, "but I expect when you are engrossed in your life as a débutante you will have no time for your father."

"You know I shall . . . always want to be . . . with you, Papa."

As she spoke, Simonetta knew she wanted to be with him now more than at any other time in her life.

Because she loved Pierre she could not bear to think of other men talking to her, dancing with her, paying her compliments.

She told herself that although she had not yet met them, she hated them already because they fell short of the ideal man she loved, the man to whom she had given her heart.

"Now we have had our fun," the Duke was saying. "On our way back to England, we must make plans carefully, Simonetta, for your presentation and for the Ball I intend to give in London towards the end of the Season."

He smiled before he said:

"I am behaving rather like an ambitious Mama, but I know it is sensible to announce that you will be having a

Ball. There will be a great number of others which will take place before yours, to which you will receive invitations on the assumption that you will invite your hostesses and their daughters back!"

"I am sure that is very wise, Papa."

The Duke smiled.

"I am determined, my dearest, that you will be a huge success, and I am quite certain that whatever Ball you attend, you will be the Belle of it!"

"I hope so . . . Papa, for . . . your sake."

"To tell the truth," the Duke continued, "I am rather looking forward to stepping back into my youth, and while you are dancing with all the eligible bachelors, I daresay I too shall find some attractive partners."

He spoke as if the idea amused him.

Simonetta wondered what he would say if she told him she had no wish to go to Balls, and that all she wanted to do was to stay at Faringham Park and paint, because in that way she would feel nearer to Pierre.

"Papa would not understand," she told herself.

She wondered further what her father would say when she made it clear that whatever advantageous proposals of marriage she received, she was determined to refuse them.

"How could I marry another man," she asked herself, "when I belong to Pierre? It would be a sacrilege to let any other man take his place in my life."

Already she could see a great many difficulties and obstacles ahead. She could almost hear not only her father arguing with her but also her aunts, and especially her Aunt Louise.

'They will never know or understand what has happened to me,' she thought despairingly.

If she revealed what had happened, her father would blame himself for having brought her abroad, although it was no fault of his that her whole outlook on life had changed.

"I suppose in a way I have grown up," Simonetta

ruminated. "When I came to Les Baux I was a child, but now I am a woman and am suffering as other women have done all through the ages."

For the first time she wondered if the Queens and Princesses in the Courts of Love had fallen in love with the Troubadours who sang to them and laid their hearts at their feet.

If so, because the love the Troubadours professed was pure and spiritual, there must have been moments in the women's lives when they felt obliged to send away a man of whom they thought they were growing too fond. Or perhaps the man was noble enough to leave them.

Until now, the Courts of Love had seemed to her like just a fantasy, where those concerned were not creatures of flesh and blood who could be both happy and also desperately, despairingly unhappy.

"You are very silent, my dearest," the Duke remarked.

"I was thinking of our time here together," Simonetta replied truthfully. "It has been very . . . revealing, Papa . . . in many ways."

"What do you mean by that?" the Duke asked.

"Les Baux has made me feel very . . . deeply, and I hope I will be a better artist because I have . . . come here," Simonetta replied, choosing her words carefully.

Her father looked surprised.

"That is what I wanted," he said. "At the same time, my dearest, I think you will have little time for painting once we open the house in London."

Simonetta did not answer.

Then as Marie came in from the kitchen to clear the table, Simonetta rose and went to sit in one of the armchairs, afraid to go to the window in case she should see the light on the rocks.

Her father fidgeted about the room, tying canvasses together and folding his easel so that he could lay it on the top of his trunk.

Simonetta watched him, thinking vaguely that he was showing himself remarkably self-sufficient, considering that at home he had his valet and innumerable other servants to perform all those tasks for him.

The Duke carried the things into his bedroom and when he came back he said:

"I am going now to the village to order a carriage to be here at seven o'clock tomorrow morning. We must leave promptly if we are to catch the eleven-o'clock train from Arles and reach Paris tomorrow evening."

"I will be ready, Papa," Simonetta said automatically.

"I will say one thing about you," the Duke remarked, "you are punctual for a woman, and that, I may tell you, is a rare virtue in those of your sex."

"I know how angry you get, Papa," Simonetta answered, "if anybody keeps you waiting!"

Her father smiled at her. Then he said:

"I will not be late, but when I have ordered the carriage I must go to the Inn to say good-bye to my friends."

"Yes, of course, Papa."

"Go to bed and have a good night. I have told Marie to call us both at six o'clock."

He did not wait for a reply but walked out through the front door, shutting it behind him.

Simonetta did not move. She merely sat in the chair, knowing there was her packing to finish upstairs and feeling not so much tired as limp and empty, as if what had happened to her this afternoon had sapped her strength and left her only a shadow of her former self.

Marie came bustling in from the kitchen.

"Is there anything else you want, *M'mselle*, before I leave?"

"No . . . thank you, Marie. We have so much enjoyed the delicious food you have prepared for us while we have been here."

"It has been delightful to cook for people who appreciate what I serve them and who are willing to pay for what is worth eating," Marie replied.

Simonetta smiled but did not say anything, and Marie went on:

"Some of those artists are like animals and gobble up anything that is set in front of them. Others, with their heads in the clouds, cannot distinguish between an oyster and a potato!"

Simonetta forced herself to laugh.

"I am sure that is true, Marie. It is called 'having an artistic temperament.'"

"Then it is something I hope I never have!" Marie retorted. "But I shall look forward to seeing you and *Monsieur* here again."

"I hope we will be able to return."

"They say those who once visit Les Baux always come back."

Simonetta thought that would not happen to her.

She had been bewitched, but not by Les Baux, except that that was where she had found Pierre.

There was no doubt that he had cast a spell over her, and the enchanted world into which he had taken her was something she could never forget and never lose.

"I am sure that is true, Marie," she said aloud, but she knew as she spoke that if she did so, Pierre would not be there.

He would never risk meeting her again, and although he might be found painting in another part of France, she would never know where it was, and his paintings would remain empty of her, just as her life would be empty of him.

"*Bonsoir, 'M'mselle,*" Marie said as she walked towards the door.

"*Bonsoir,* Marie!"

Simonetta heard Marie moving about the kitchen and then there was the sound of the back-door shutting and her heavy footsteps going round the house and down the garden path to the little gate.

As soon as she was alone, Simonetta put her head

back against the armchair, closed her eyes, and thought on Pierre.

Only to think of him made the agony of losing him worse than it was already, and yet it was impossible to think of anything else.

She went back over the time when they had first met; the things they had said to each other; the moment when she had become tinglingly aware of him as a man; the moment when she had longed for him to kiss her; and how abruptly he had walked ahead towards the house.

"I wanted him to kiss me then as I have never wanted anything before," Simonetta murmured.

Then there was again the magic of their kiss when he had carried her up into the sky, and everything she had ever imagined or dreamt about love had been but a pale imitation of the ecstatic, glorious reality.

Now she understood why love made men fight wars for the women they loved and made women willing to go to the stake with their lovers without screaming or protesting.

She understood, almost as if somebody were giving her a lecture, how artists had been inspired to write music that thrilled those who listened to it and how writers had inscribed poems for those they loved, which had entranced other women all down the ages.

Love! Love! Love!

Although it was an agony as well as a rapture, Simonetta knew that no-one had lived unless they had loved as she loved Pierre.

She must have sat for a long time thinking of him, so long in fact that when she opened her eyes she realised that the room was in darkness and night had come.

Outside, the stars filled the sky and the moon was shining on the rocks, but she knew she could not bear to look at the silver loveliness of it as she had done with Pierre.

She rose slowly to her feet, thinking that she must go

upstairs and finish her packing so that she would be ready to leave with her father in the morning.

It was then that she noticed that the window opposite her, which was beside the front door, was wide open and she thought she should shut it.

At the same time, she was determined to look as little as possible at the moonlight.

She walked across the room, putting out her hands in front of her so that she did not stumble over the chairs, and thinking vaguely that she would have to light the candles in her bedroom so as to finish her packing.

She reached the window, and as she did so she heard the sound of wheels.

It flashed through her mind that it was the carriage which her father had ordered to take them to Arles.

Then she knew that was absurd, for it was night and not morning.

She leant out on the window-sill and saw to her surprise that there was a carriage approaching, and as she watched, it came to a standstill outside the garden gate.

It was drawn by two horses and there were two men on the box, and as it stopped, one of the men jumped down and ran round to open the door.

As he did so, another man appeared from amongst the bushes at the end of the garden.

Hardly aware of what she was doing, Simonetta watched him moving through the flowers until he reached the carriage.

It was impossible for Simonetta to see their faces, for the moon was not yet shining directly on this lower part of the valley, and all she was aware of was the outline of the carriage and the dim figures of the men.

Although the man who had come through the garden spoke in a whisper, she found that in the stillness of the night she could hear what he said.

"The man's left, but the girl is still indoors, *Monsieur Comte.*"

For a moment the meaning of the words did not percolate Simonetta's mind, but then when it did, she felt her heart stand still.

She was caught in a trap!

Panic-stricken, she knew that the man in the carriage was the *Comte* and the two men speaking to him were his servants.

For a moment it was impossible to breathe or even to move.

Then as the full significance of what she had heard swept over her, the fear that came with it was almost as if she had been struck by lightning.

He had said that when she left Les Baux he would take her to Paris with him, and that was what he now had come to do, with or without her consent.

Just for a second, all Simonetta could think of was to scream from sheer terror. Then her intelligence told her that she somehow must escape.

Even as she thought of it she heard the *Comte* say in a very low voice, which, however, she could hear:

"Go in through the back-door, Jean, and you, Gustav, through the front."

It was then that Simonetta was aware that she had only a second in which to save herself.

Moving swiftly in her thin slippers which made no sound, she turned from the window towards the stairs, and even as she did so she knew that there she would be trapped.

"Oh, God, help me!" she prayed.

Almost as if a voice directed her, she was aware that there was only one thing she could do.

She entered her father's bedroom, crossed it, and went into the small toilette where she had bathed.

It had a small window which looked out at the back of the house, and it took only a moment for Simonetta to open it.

Because she was used to mounting her own horses without help, climbing trees, and finding five-bar gates no obstacle, she swung herself onto the window-sill and squeezed through the window.

There was only a short drop down onto the soft earth beneath, and as she landed on the ground she could hear the footsteps of one of the *Comte*'s servants going up the stairs towards her bedroom.

It was then that frantically she began to run through the bushes which lay behind the house and which after a short distance gave way to a small copse of olive and cypress trees.

Once she was amongst them it was impossible to move quickly, first because there was a great deal of undergrowth, and secondly because the trees obscured the moonlight.

She had to hold her hands out in front of her to prevent herself from bumping into them, and her movements were encumbered by weeds and briars.

She moved as quickly as she could, terrified that at any second she might hear the *Comte*'s men searching for her.

It would be only a question of time before they would guess that because the window of the *toilette* was opened, that was the way she had escaped.

She felt her heart beating wildly with her fear, and her lips were dry, while her breath was coming in frightened gasps through her parted lips.

'If the *Comte* takes me away,' she thought, 'it will be a long time before Papa finds out what has happened to me.'

She began to wish that she had told her father of how the *Comte* had behaved with her and what he had suggested.

The Duke had disliked the compliments he had paid her, but he had no idea that he was so determined to possess her that he was prepared to take her by force if necessary.

'It might be weeks or months before I am rescued,' Simonetta thought, 'and by then it will be . . . too late.'

She did not quite understand what was meant by "too late." She knew only that the *Comte* would touch her and kiss her, and because he was a strong man while she was small, there would be little she could do about it.

The idea was horrifying, disgusting, and at the same time so degrading that she thought that if he did touch her she must die, although she had no idea how she could kill herself.

She knew she was frightened to the point where, like a small animal escaping from a fox or a prowling tiger, she must run and run until she dropped through sheer exhaustion.

The trees were coming to an end and she knew that when they did so she would be in the field where Pierre and she had been this afternoon.

It flashed through her mind that perhaps by some miracle he would still be there.

Then she knew despairingly that there was no chance of that.

It was too dark to paint, and she felt that he would not want to look at the moonlight because it would remind him of their happiness.

But somehow she must find either Pierre or her father, or she would be captured by the *Comte* and lost forever.

"What can I . . . do?" she asked herself as she pushed her way through the trees. "Where can . . . I . . . go?"

She felt that the briars that clung round her ankles were allies of the *Comte* and were holding her back, imprisoning her.

'If only I had stayed at home instead of taking part in this mad charade with Papa, I would be safe,' she thought.

The calm serenity of Faringham Park seemed now like a haven which she would never see again.

Then she was through the trees and running over the grassland where she had run so joyously towards Pierre.

She was almost at the very place where he had set up his easel, and as she reached it she thought she heard a man shout in the distance behind her.

The sound seemed to streak through her breast with an irrepressible terror so that she stifled a scream from her lips and ran even more frantically towards the Temple of Love.

She had a sudden, wild hope that perhaps the men would not search for her there, or that if she lay down on the floor in the darkness they might not see her.

The ground was very rough and every step seemed more difficult than the last, and she was gasping for breath by the time she reached the Temple.

It seemed for the moment the only place of safety she could reach, and yet she was terribly afraid that she would be seen before she could hide.

Then as she went in through the entrance she realised it was not empty: there was something large and dark inside, and she gave a scream of sheer terror.

Then suddenly, so suddenly that she could hardly believe it was happening, Pierre's arms were round her, holding her, and his voice was almost like the voice of God, who had come to save her, as he said:

"*Ma chérie!* My darling! What has happened?"

It was impossible for Simonetta to answer.

She could only collapse against him, semi-conscious now from the ordeal she had been through.

He lifted her in his arms and carried her farther inside the small Temple. Then as he held her closely against him they sat down together on a stone seat.

"What has happened?" Pierre asked again, and she could hear the anxiety in his voice. "You must tell me."

She was still breathless and exhausted, but as if he compelled her she managed to say in a voice that did not sound like her own:

"Th-the *Comte* . . .! The *Comte* . . . he came to the . . . h-house to t-take me . . . away!"

"*Mon Dieu!* But this is intolerable!" Pierre exclaimed.

He made a movement as if he would rise, but because Simonetta was now more frightened for him than for herself, she held on to him, saying:

"No . . . no! He has . . . two men with . . . him. He said he would . . . take me to . . . Paris and . . . that is what he . . . intends to . . . do."

As she spoke she realised that by this time the men might be searching amongst the trees and would soon find her and Pierre.

"They are . . . f-following me," she said. "They will find us . . . and they will h-hurt you."

Pierre's arms tightened round her and she knew he was thinking.

"I do not think they will find us here," he said after a moment, "and if they come from between the trees, we should be able to see them. I could take you to the village, but I think it would be a mistake."

He spoke as if he was thinking aloud, and Simonetta, still finding it hard to breathe, could only hold on to him and try to believe that she had no longer to run away since now she had Pierre to protect her.

She realised that he was watching the wood, and after a moment she said:

"Suppose they . . . both come?"

"I should be able to manage two men," Pierre replied. "But it is the *Comte* I would like to fight."

"Oh . . . no . . . you must no do . . . that!" Simonetta said. "It will make a great deal of . . . trouble for you, and already I am . . . afraid he will somehow . . . prevent you from . . . selling your paintings."

"You are still thinking of me?"

"How can I think of . . . anybody else?" Simonetta said with a sob in her voice.

He held her closer still before he said:

"I cannot understand how this has happened."

"My . . . Master went to the . . . village to order a carriage . . . we leave tomorrow."

"Tomorrow? But you had no intention of leaving when I talked to you this afternoon."

"No . . . but he has to return . . . suddenly to . . . England."

As she spoke she thought how surprised Pierre would be if she explained why her father had to return, but apparently he was not curious, and after a moment he said:

"It solves one problem. Once you have gone back to your own country, you should be safe from the *Comte*."

"Y-yes . . . that is . . . true," Simonetta agreed.

She knew as she spoke that Pierre had no idea that the *Comte* would find it very difficult to believe that the "Art Student" whom he expected to be able to abduct without there being any trouble about it was a well-protected young lady of fashion and the daughter of a Duke.

"If he comes anywhere near you," Pierre went on, "you are to go at once to the Police—do you understand? Or surely you have a relative who would do this for you?"

"Yes . . . I have . . . relatives in . . . England."

"I wish I could speak to them and tell them how carefully they must look after you. And never again—never, never!—do you understand, Simonetta?—are you to go away to France with an elderly man who cannot protect you properly."

"That is unfair!" Simonetta said, feeling she must stand up for her father.

"Perhaps it is," Pierre agreed. "But you are too beautiful, my little Venus, that is the whole trouble, and there will always be men who will pursue you—"

He paused before he said:

"Oh God! How can I allow such a thing to happen to you? How can I leave you and be tortured day and night thinking of men like the *Comte* threatening you and making you as frightened as you are now?"

"I . . . I would have been very . . . very frightened if you had not . . . been here."

As she spoke she raised her head to look towards the wood.

Now the moonlight had turned the field in front of them into shimmering silver, and to the right and left of them the rocks were dark purple except where the moonlight touched the tops of them with a flowing, luminous light.

It was beautiful, and yet because of the *Comte* at the same time it was sinister. Simonetta's fingers tightened as she held on to Pierre, and he could feel her whole slender body trembling against him.

"It is no use, my precious one," he said in a voice deep with emotion that seemed to vibrate through her. "I cannot leave you, and the only way I can protect and look after you is by marrying you!"

This was something Simonetta had not expected him to say.

She looked up at him in surprise, and for a moment she forgot the menace of the *Comte* and his men searching for her.

Then she knew that although Pierre had said the words she wanted to hear and the joy of it was already running through her body like little shafts of sunlight, she had to refuse him.

But before she could speak, Pierre went on:

"It is not going to be easy for you. In fact I am telling you the truth when I say it will be very difficult for you to be my wife, and perhaps you will be unhappy."

He drew in his breath and continued:

"I swear I will do everything in my power to prevent you from being hurt, although I know that at times it will be impossible for me to prevent it."

"I . . . I do not . . . understand."

She knew she should tell him that such an idea was impossible anyway, but for the moment the words would not come to her lips.

At the same time, she could not help being curious as to why he thought she would be unhappy.

"Why . . . should I be . . . unhappy?" she asked.

"You are English and French families, as you must know, are very different from English ones. Mine, my darling, will be furious at my marrying you, and since it will be too late to prevent you from becoming my wife, they will do all they can to make you realise that they do not want you, that they reject you and disapprove of the life you lived before we met."

His answer was not at all what Simonetta had expected.

She had thought he would say he was offering her a life of poverty and the endless difficulties of earning a living by his painting.

She stared up at him, trying to make sense of what he had said, conscious at the same time of the wonder of knowing that he wanted her as his wife, and that although he had never spoken of it before, he had now asked her to marry him.

"You see, my beautiful one," Pierre explained, "although you feared that the *Comte* would prevent me from selling my paintings, that anxiety was quite unnecessary."

"W-why?" Simonetta asked.

"Because I am not an artist, except in my spare time."

"N-not an . . . artist? . . . But I thought . . . "

"I love painting," Pierre said. "I love it, and I want—although sometimes I am afraid it is an impossible ambition—to be a good Impressionist."

"But surely . . . you will be one?"

She knew he smiled as he looked down at her.

"That is what I want you to think, and your opinion is the only one that matters. Actually, darling, it would be very much easier if you were in fact marrying an Impressionist."

He kissed her forehead and went on:

"All we would have to do then would be to struggle to

live, and sell the paintings which I feel you will inspire me to paint as well as the artist whom you admire so much—Claude Monet."

"And Sisley," Simonetta murmured.

She thought of the beautiful painting she had seen by him at the *Comte's château*.

As if even to think of the *Comte* brought back the fear he had aroused in her, she moved so that she could see the whole length of the field.

It was dark, but in the moonlight there appeared to be no men lurking in the darkness, but if there were, they were certainly not approaching the Temple.

"Forget the *Comte,*" Pierre said. "By now he will have acknowledged that he has lost you and he will drive away out of our lives forever."

"Do you . . . do you really . . . think he will . . . do that?"

"I believe that however conceited or presumptuous he may be, he will not risk following you to the village, where he will imagine you have gone."

"I hope you are . . . right."

"Now let us talk about ourselves," Pierre said. "I have made up my mind and I should have done so before. We will be married, and although my family are not as formidable as the *Comte,* you will find them very difficult."

His arms rightened round her.

"But we will face them together, and I promise that in time, with your beauty, your charm, and, my adorable one, your intelligent little mind, you will win them over."

"I cannot quite see . . . why they should be . . . against me."

"It will not be because of you personally. It is because in my family an Art Student is so foreign to their lives that they will consider such a person beneath their notice, and therefore they will deeply resent my marrying one."

Simonetta drew in her breath.

"It is very . . . wonderful of you to want to . . . marry me, and . . . Pierre . . . you will not understand . . . b-but I have to say . . . 'no'!"

She thought he would ask her why, and she was wondering frantically what he would say, when he gave a sudden laugh and held her against him.

"You are thinking of me again, and I love you for it. Could anybody be more wonderful, more unselfish? But I promise you, it is quite unnecessary."

For the first time since she had come to him his lips touched hers and he kissed her before he said:

"I do not intend to listen to any arguments. You are mine, and I intend to marry you. You will be my wife, and, darling, whatever difficulties we encounter, when we come here the magic of our love will make us completely immune to anything anybody can say or do to hurt us."

"Oh, Pierre, I . . . I cannot . . . marry you!" Simonetta cried. "And . . . please . . . you must . . . listen to me before you say . . . any more."

"This afternoon," he said as if she had not spoken, "I sent you away because I was thinking of you and I could not bear that you should be unhappy. Now I know that you are not safe unless I am there."

Once again he kissed her and silenced the words she was trying to say.

"Because I know," he went on, "that for us to be apart is completely and absolutely impossible, we will be married immediately, and when you are my wife I will protect you, love you, and worship you for as long as we both shall live."

It was a vow, and because it was so moving, for the moment Simonetta could not speak.

Then as the agony she was suffering increased, she knew she would have to tell Pierre of her deception and that however deep their love was, however much she needed him, she would never be allowed to marry him.

She drew in her breath, knowing how hard it was even to begin to say such things, but Pierre spoke first.

"You see, my darling," he said, "I am not Pierre Valéry as you believe. My real name is Montreuil, and I am actually the *Duc* de Montreuil!"

Simonetta stiffened as if turned to stone.

She could not believe what she had heard, and she thought she was dreaming.

Then as if the silence was more than Pierre could bear he said:

"Now you know the truth, and I do not want you to be afraid. It will mean that wherever we live and whatever we do, as my wife I will love and protect you."

He bent his head to find her lips, but Simonetta gave a little gasp that was almost a laugh. Then suddenly she began to cry.

She had held back her tears for so long, but finally the relief after all she had suffered broke her self-control.

Tears streamed down her cheeks and she hid her face against Pierre's shoulder and wept tempestuously.

Chapter Seven

"It is all right, my darling. It is all right!" Pierre kept saying as Simonetta tried unsuccessfully to control her tears.

They were tears of relief and they swept away the misery, the frustration, and the despair which had been so agonising all the evening.

With her terror of the *Comte* to bear in addition, she felt as if she had run through every emotion possible to a human being.

Now it was over and she could not believe it.

"It is all right," Pierre said again. "We will be married, and I will never allow my little Venus to be unhappy again."

"I am . . . happy," Simonetta managed to stammer. "I am . . . happy, Pierre . . . but I thought it would be . . . impossible for me to . . . m-marry you."

"You will be my wife," he said, "and I will never allow you to cry like this again."

He turned her face up to his. Then he was kissing away the tears from her eyes, her cheeks, and lastly her mouth.

At the touch of his lips Simonetta felt thrill after thrill flash through her, and it was like coming back to life from the dead.

Once again he was carrying her up into the sky and there was the rapture and wonder of being close to him, of belonging to him.

"I love . . . you . . . I love you . . . I love . . . you," her heart was saying.

Then Pierre raised his head, and vaguely, far away at the back of her mind, Simonetta remembered that she must now tell him why she could marry him, and who she was.

"P-Pierre . . . " she began.

At that moment she heard footsteps on the road.

She stiffened and knew that Pierre did too, and it flashed through both their minds that one of the *Comte's* men had found them.

Then in the roadway coming from the direction of the village Simonetta could see the tall figure of her father.

Quickly she moved from Pierre's arms and leaning through the open trellis-work of the Temple called:

"Papa! Papa!"

Her voice was low, for she was still apprehensive that the *Comte* might be outside the house.

As she spoke she was aware that Pierre had stiffened, while her father had stopped dead in the middle of the road.

"Papa!" Simonetta said again in a voice even lower than it had been before.

"Simonetta?" the Duke queried. "Where are you? What are you doing out here?"

Simonetta stepped out of the Temple.

As she did so, her father walked towards her and crossed the lavender hedge to come to her side.

"What has happened? Why have you not gone to bed?"

Then as Pierre appeared behind Simonetta, he asked sharply:

"Who is this?"

Simonetta held on to her father's arm.

"Listen, Papa," she said. "After you had gone to the village, the *Comte* de Laval... arrived in a carriage with two men, and he... intended to... take me... away with... him by force."

Her voice faltered as she spoke.

She knew that her father was staring at her incredulously, as if he could not believe what he had heard.

"Take you away with him?" he asked, his voice rising. "What the Devil do you mean by that?"

Simonetta's hand tightened on his arm.

"Not... so loud... Papa! The *Comte* and his men may... still be in the house. I had to... climb out of a window... and because I was so... terrified... the *Duc* de Montreuil... protected me."

"I have never heard such a story!" the Duke said angrily.

"It is true, Sir," Pierre said quietly.

The Duke looked up at him as he stood on the steps of the little Temple. Then he said:

"You are the *Duc* de Montreuil? Then it must have been your father I knew. We often met racing."

Simonetta saw the surprise on Pierre's face, and there was a touch of laughter in her voice as she said a little unsteadily, as if she was still not far from tears:

"I have... not told the *Duc* who... we are."

"There is no reason why he should know," the Duke said, as if he resented breaking his incognito. "But if he has been kind enough to protect you from that swine de Laval, I am certainly very grateful."

"So am... I," Simonetta murmured.

"Thank you," the Duke said to Pierre, "and although I have no wish for it to be known here in Les Baux, I am the Duke of Faringham!"

There was now such a look of astonishment on Pierre's face that it made Simonetta laugh.

It was only a choking little sound, but she felt as if it

were a paean of gratitude which swept her up into the starlit sky where a celestial choir of angels sang songs of love like those of the Troubadours.

* * *

Simonetta stood in her bedroom looking at herself in the mirror and wondering if Pierre would think she was beautiful enough to bear his name.

She had sent away the Housekeeper and the maids who had been dressing her, because she was early and her father was not yet ready to take her to the Chapel.

She wanted to be alone for a few minutes to think of the happiness that was waiting for her.

A happiness that she had thought would never be hers.

Now it seemed like a marvellous fairy-story and all the difficulties of their being married had been swept away as if by a magic wand.

She could understand how apprehensive Pierre had been of his family's anger and disappointment if he married an Art Student, just as she knew that her father would have refused categorically to give his consent to her marrying an Impressionist painter.

Pierre's family were aristocratic, exceedingly proud, and fanatically protective of their heritage.

If she had arrived at the Castle in Normandy married to the head of the family, they would have vied with one another to give his wife, whom they would have considered he had picked up in the gutter, a life of misery.

'Even if I were with Pierre, it would have been intolerable to be sneered at, scorned, and treated with contempt every day of my life,' Simonetta thought.

But as a Duke's daughter, with a family as distinguished in England as the de Montreuils were in France, they had welcomed Simonetta with open arms.

They made no secret of the fact that they were delighted that Pierre was to be married at last and the family would carry on as it had done since the days of King Charlemagne.

"It seems unfair," Simonetta said, "because whatever my fame might be, I would still be me."

"I am convinced, my precious one," Pierre answered, "that in time they would have grown to love you. But human nature is human nature, and if we can take convenient short-cuts to happiness, let us always be prepared to take them."

Simonetta had laughed. Then she said:

"While you were determined not to marry me, I knew that I, for my part, would never be allowed to marry Pierre Valéry."

"I think eventually," Pierre replied, "even if all the world were aligned against us, love would have triumphed, because, my darling, it has a power that is greater than anything else."

He put his arms round her and went on:

"I personally am prepared to go down on my knees and thank God, fate, and even the *Comte,* that we discovered before it was too late that we can be married with the blessing of all those who love us."

Simonetta gave a little cry.

"Supposing . . . just supposing you had . . . gone away! Then even if the *Comte* had not . . . carried me away to Paris, Papa would have . . . taken me back to . . . England and I would . . . never have . . . seen you again!"

Pierre's arms tightened round her until it was almost impossible for her to breathe.

"You are not to think about it," he commanded. "You are mine, and if any man ever again tries to touch you, I swear I will murder him!"

Then he was kissing her passionately, fiercely, demandingly, so that his lips hurt hers, and she knew it was because he was afraid that he might have lost her.

It had been very difficult to explain to her father that the *Duc* de Montreuil, who had saved her from the *Comte* and whom she was supposed to have met for the first time that evening, was a man she loved with all her heart and wanted to marry.

Her father and Pierre had gone cautiously back to the house ahead of her to see if the *Comte* had given up the chase and gone home.

Finding that this was what he had done, they had a drink together, and after they had also expressed forcefully and volubly what they felt about the *Comte*'s appalling behaviour, they became friends.

What was more, they all left Les Baux the next morning in the same carriage and travelled in the same train to Paris.

There, while the *Duc* had gone to stay at his own house, which he admitted was only partially open, the Duke had insisted that he and Simonetta should stay in the same quiet Hotel where they had stayed before.

"I have no wish to see any of my acquaintances while I am dressed like this," the Duke had said, "and what is more, I am very anxious not to break my incognito in France. Otherwise I shall never again be able to come here and paint with my Impressionist friends, which is something I so much enjoy doing."

"I do understand," Pierre had said with a smile. "I have learnt so much from them because they have accepted me as Pierre Valéry, and they would never in a thousand years be at ease or friendly with the *Duc* de Montreuil."

Both men had laughed, and only when Pierre had said good-bye did Simonetta say:

"The *Duc* was saying, Papa, how much he would like to see our paintings at home. Could you not invite him to come and stay before we have to go to London?"

"Of course," the Duke agreed, "but I am afraid it will have to be almost immediately, as Simonetta is to be presented at Court at the beginning of next month."

"To tell the truth," Pierre replied, "I was trying to find an opportunity of inviting myself to Faringham

Park to see your collection of paintings, which of course is world-famous. I am also enormously interested in your own paintings."

The Duke was delighted, and when Pierre said he would arrive at Faringham Park in four days' time, did not notice the light in his daughter's eyes.

Luckily, he also missed noticing that she had slipped her hand into Pierre's and he squeezed her fingers almost bloodless.

In four days' time Pierre arrived at Faringham Park, and the very first afternoon when Simonetta took him out riding to show him some of the Estate they stopped in the woods.

Leaving their horses tethered to a fallen tree, they stood looking at each other until Simonetta melted into Pierre's arms.

He kissed her until she was breathless and her feet were no longer on the ground. She felt she was not in the familiar woods at home but in the light that had shone on the rocks of Les Baux.

"I love you! God—how I love you!" he said when it was possible to speak. "We cannot go on like this. I am going to ask your father tonight if he will give him permission for me to marry you."

"It is . . . too . . . soon."

Pierre groaned.

"It felt like four centuries to me before I could see you again. If you think I can go back to France and wait any longer for you to become my wife, you are very much mistaken."

Simonetta laughed as she said:

"I am sure if you speak to Papa as an Impressionist, he will understand that love at first sight is just as possible as the fact that there is no black on an Impressionist's palette."

Pierre laughed too. Then he said:

"Oh, my darling, how can we be so fortunate, so

unbelievably lucky? I do not have to worry over your
being made unhappy by my family or that your father
thinks I am not good enough for his daughter."

He kissed her before he added:

"In fact, of course, I am not good enough! No-one in
the world could be good enough for someone as beautiful and perfect as you, my precious little love. But
believe me, no man could love you more than I do."

"Oh, Pierre, I love you so much, and I too am
grateful. Please... please... let us be... married
very... very... soon."

The Duke was at first surprised that everything had
happened so quickly, but Pierre was very eloquent in
declaring the he could not endure the torture of jealou-
sy or the fear that Simonetta might forget him if she did
a Season in London and found somebody she loved
more than she loved him.

Apart from the fact that the Duke felt his daughter
had made the right choice, he was well aware that the
Duc de Montreuil was a very rich man and had large,
important Estates in France.

In fact, Pierre was a matrimonial catch whom any
parent would be pleased to welcome as a son-in-law.

But that was immaterial beside the fact that the Duke
could see that Simonetta was deeply in love and he had
never known her to be so happy.

Finally, he surrendered. Pierre had his way and the
wedding was arranged for three weeks after Simonetta
had made her curtsey at Buckingham Palace.

The de Montreuil relations poured over from France
to be present, but because they were Catholic, the
actual Ceremony was to be a small private one in the
Chapel at Faringham Park.

It had originally been consecrated by a Catholic
Archbishop when the house was first built as part of a
Cistercian Monastery.

As a special dispensation from the Pope, it was
allowed to be used again by the Roman Catholic Cardi-

nal who arrived from London to conduct the marriage.

While the preparations were being made, Simonetta said to Pierre when they were alone:

"Because I love you, darling Pierre, and because I know it will please you and your family, once we are married I would like to be received into your Church."

He stared at her for a moment incredulously. Then he said in a low voice:

"Do you really mean that?"

"I think . . . whatever we call ourselves . . . to you and me, God is the same. He has looked after us, brought us together, and made us happy."

"Of course He is the same," Pierre answered, "and I am deeply touched, my darling, that you should wish to become a Catholic."

"I want to do what you do, believe in what you believe, and to worship beside you."

Because he was deeply moved, Pierre could only raise her hand to his lips, and having kissed it he said:

"There are no words for me to tell you how wonderful you are!"

Now, looking at herself in the mirror, Simonetta was aware that while the Chapel held only their immediate and closest relatives, the guests for the Reception were already arriving in the Ball-Room.

As it was a brilliant, sunny afternoon, many of them were walking outside in the garden while they drank Champagne and waited for her and Pierre to appear.

Later they were to cut the four-tiered wedding-cake which the cooks had been frantically icing and decorating for the past week.

In the Park was a huge marquee where all the employees, the tenant-farmers, and the villagers were assembling to drink beer and cider and to eat an enormous meal of roasted ox, boar's head, and venison.

There would be speeches, and hundreds of hands to shake and good wishes to listen to.

But Simonetta was thinking only of the moment when she and Pierre would drive away from it and be alone.

She knew they would stay tonight on their way to Dover at a house which had been lent to them by one of her relatives.

Then tomorrow they would cross the Channel and be in France.

After that, Pierre had refused to tell her where they were going, but she guessed it was where there would be the light which meant so much to them, and she was sure that that meant Provence.

It would not be in Les Baux, because that was too redolent of memories of the *Comte*, but she had the feeling that they would not be far away.

Then, safe in his arms, together they could see the light which, as Pierre had said, had moved through their eyes and into their hearts and souls and was now an indivisible part of themselves.

"He is so wonderful!" Simonetta whispered to herself.

There was a knock on the door.

It meant that her father was waiting for her and was ready to take her downstairs to the Chapel.

"I am just coming."

As she spoke she pulled her veil over her face.

As it fell below her waist at the front and hung over her train at the back, she thought for one moment that it made her seem almost like a ghost of herself.

Then she hoped that instead that she looked ethereal, like the apparition from another world which Pierre had thought she must be when she first appeared in the Temple of Love.

There was a smile on her lips as she picked up her bouquet and moved towards the door.

* * *

It was very quiet in the darkness as Simonetta pushed back the sheet that covered her and rose from the bed with its silk hangings.

On bare feet she walked silently across the thick carpet towards the window, and pulling aside one of the heavy velvet curtains looked out.

As she expected, the view in front of her was silver in the moonlight.

The trees on the other side of the lake were dark with deep purple shadows beneath them, while the lake itself was molten silver and glittered with the reflection of the stars.

She stood looking at the beauty of it. Then a voice said:

"*Ma chérie*, I want you."

"I thought you were asleep."

"How can I sleep when all I can think about is you?" Pierre answered.

She turned to smile at him, and as she did so she was silhouetted in the moonlight which haloed her hair and the radiance of her face.

Pierre could also see her slim body beneath the transparency of her nightgown.

"Come here," he said softly.

"No. Come and look at the moonlight, Pierre, it is so beautiful! It is as lovely as it was when we saw it together at Les Baux."

She turned once again to the window and said, almost as if she was speaking to herself:

"I think the moonlight will always mean something very precious to us! I was certain when we sat beneath the Castle that you carried me up to the stars."

As she finished speaking she gave a little start, for although she had not heard him move, Pierre was beside her.

His arms went round her and she leant back against him, saying:

"Look! Is it not beautiful?"

"I am looking at you," he replied, "and you are the most beautiful sight I have ever seen! But you are also my wife, and I am jealous when you are not thinking of me."

Simonetta laughed. Then she said:

"You would grow very conceited if you knew how much I think of you and how it is impossible to think of anything else."

"And yet you are disobedient," Pierre replied. "I told you to come to me."

"I wanted to see the moonlight."

"I am not interested in the moonlight but in you, my adorable, wonderful, exciting little Venus!"

As he spoke he turned her round, and as his lips found hers he lifted her up in his arms and carried her back to the bed.

He put her down gently, then he was beside her, holding her close against him, kissing her eyes, her cheeks, her straight little nose, and lastly her lips.

He felt her draw a little closer as she responded to him. Then she said with a little catch in her voice:

"Oh, Pierre . . . I love . . . you! I had no idea that love could be so . . . overwhelming . . . so powerful . . . and yet so . . . tender and so . . . gentle."

"You were not frightened, my precious?"

"How could you ever frighten me? To me you mean safety, and I know that as long as I am in your arms, no enemy could ever . . . hurt me."

"I hope that is true," he said quietly.

"It . . . is."

Then as his hands moved over her body he said:

"I am still afraid that you might vanish as I expected you to do the first time I saw you."

"And I was so afraid that you might . . . leave me, as you . . . tried to do," Simonetta answered. "Then I would have been . . . left only with our . . . moments of love to . . . remember."

There was a note in her voice that told Pierre how much she had suffered when she thought she would never see him again and that it was still an unhealed scar within her.

He drew her closer and said:

"Now all our moments have melted into one, my darling, my precious little wife, and those moments of love we were going to treasure apart from each other have become one great moment when we will live together and love each other and nothing else will be of any importance in our lives. Do you believe that?"

"I want to believe it," Simonetta answered, "and yet even today, our wedding-day . . . I was afraid that . . . something might sweep us . . . apart and I would . . . lose you."

She paused before she added:

"Or perhaps you would . . . change your mind at the . . . last moment and no longer . . . love me."

Pierre laughed, and it seemed almost like a flash of light in the darkness.

"Oh, my sweet," he said, "that is as impossible as that the stars should fall from the sky, or the moon cease to shine. Have you forgotten that we are Impressionists? We have found the light and now it is ours forever."

"Forever," Simonetta whispered.

"Today, tomorrow, for eternity, I shall love you, adore you, and worship you, and our special light will grow and increase until it is there forever to guide us up into the skies."

Simonetta gave a little cry.

"Oh, Pierre, if that is what you believe . . . then I believe it too, and I love you! I love you with . . . all my heart and soul!"

"As I love you," Pierre replied, "and you are mine."

His lips moved over the softness of her cheek towards her mouth as he said:

"Your heart, your soul, your adorable enquiring little

mind, and also your exciting body are all mine, my precious!"

Then his lips were on hers and she felt the fire rising in him and knew that this too was a part of their love.

She felt a flame flicker within her, rising up through her breast and into her throat until it reached her lips.

Then as they drew closer and closer, the moonlight outside seemed to be joined with the luminous light that came from themselves, and in the moment of love they were lifted up on the wings of ecstasy to the stars.

ABOUT THE AUTHOR

BARBARA CARTLAND is the bestselling authoress in the world, according to the *Guinness Book of World Records*. She has sold over 200 million books and has beaten the world record for five years running, last year with 24 and the previous years with 24, 20, and 23.

She is also an historian, playwright, lecturer, political speaker and television personality, and has now written over 320 books.

She has also had many historical works published and has written four autobiographies as well as the biographies of her mother and that of her brother, Ronald Cartland, who was the first Member of Parliament to be killed in the last war. This book has a preface by Sir Winston Churchill and has just been republished with an introduction by Sir Arthur Bryant.

Love at the Helm, a novel written with the help and inspiration of the late Earl Mountbatten of Burma, Uncle of His Royal Highness Prince Philip, is being sold for the Mountbatten Memorial Trust.

In 1978 Miss Cartland sang an Album of Love Songs with the Royal Philharmonic Orchestra.

She is unique in that she was #1 and #2 in the Dalton List of Bestsellers, and one week had four books in the top twenty.

In private life Barbara Cartland, who is a Dame of the Order of St. John of Jerusalem, Chairman of the St. John Council in Hertfordshire and Deputy President of the St. John Ambulance Brigade, has also fought for better conditions and salaries for midwives and nurses.

As President of the Royal College of Midwives (Hertfordshire Branch) she has been invested with the first badge of Office ever given in Great Britain, which was subscribed to by the midwives themselves.

Barbara Cartland is deeply interested in vitamin therapy and is President of the British National Association for Health. Her book, *The Magic of Honey*, has sold throughout the world and is translated into many languages.

She has a magazine "Barbara Cartland's World of Romance" now being published in the USA.